Carson Kettle US Marshal
Carson Kettle United States Marshal - Book 3

by

Wyatt Cochrane

This book is a work of fiction. Names, characters, places, and incidents are products of the author's imagination or are used fictitiously. Any resemblance to actual events or persons, living or dead, is entirely coincidental.

© Copyright 2021 — Wyatt Cochrane

All rights reserved. Other than brief quotes included for the purposes of reviews, no part of this book may be reproduced by any means without prior written consent of the author.

DEDICATION

To Marie, for all she does for me and for our family. And for the invaluable assistance she provides in the creation of these books.

CHAPTER one

Carson couldn't remember the last time he'd had this much fun with his brothers, or anyone else for that matter. He grasped the coarse, thick rope and climbed the bank as high as he could, while still leaving enough tail to allow him to reach up, hang on, and plant his feet on the big knot in the end of the heavy hemp.

He leaned back and counted, "One. Two. Three." Then launched himself into space.

The rope arced down, its frayed tail just brushing the sparkling Arkansas River before climbing high over the deep pool. Carson hung from his arms and grabbed at the knot with his toes, but only succeeded in knocking it away.

As he reached the highest point in the swing, he let go with his hands, tried to spin his body in the air and enter the water headfirst, the way his little brother George had just done.

With no push from his legs, his arms and legs flailed. He tore his gaze from the only wispy cloud in the bluebird sky and tried to lean his head back enough to find the water with his eyes.

He hit the water flat on his back with a slap louder than an alarmed beaver's tail. The air whooshed from his lungs. How could something as soft and fluid as river water hit so hard?

As he sank below the surface of the cool river, he fought to suck in a breath, but his lungs refused to cooperate and all he got was a mouthful of muddy water. He rolled over onto his belly and kicked himself to the surface.

His three younger brothers, George, Able, and Will, swam toward him. All three laughing and splashing water his way.

His cheeks burned as he tried to tell them it wasn't one bit funny, but his frozen lungs only released enough air to let him croak.

George, tears streaming from his merry eyes, arrived first, grabbed one arm, and towed him toward the shallows.

As his middle relaxed and he was about to speak, he glanced up at the bank he had just launched from.

The new deputy, Marty Dunnegan, stood near the clothes-decorated hickory, a huge grin on his face, slowly clapping his hands. Clap! Clap! Clap! Deputy Marty Dunnegan was short and broad, with a shock of red hair poking from under his hat, and a face full of freckles.

Carson's feet found the slick mud of the river bottom. He stood, shook his head, and started toward the bank. Marshal Greer had insisted he take three days at home before returning to Fort Smith and preparing for a trip back to arrest the men he'd been forced to leave north of Rocky Comfort. It had only been one day, but Marty wouldn't be here if Marshal Greer hadn't sent him.

Marty grabbed his belly and doubled over in laughter. "Water must be cold, Kettle."

Carson covered his privates with both hands. With his sister, Katy, away at a friend's, he and his brothers had hung their clothes... all their clothes... on a hickory limb.

Carson's face burned. Shaking his head, he climbed the slick bank and pulled his red union suit from the branch.

"What is it?" Carson asked.

Marty looked past him. "Marshal wants you."

"Figured as much. What's happened?"

Marty glanced over Carson's shoulder at his brothers, still smiling and following him up the bank. "Don't know. When I went to the office this morning, Marshal Greer just looked up and said, 'Go find Kettle and bring him back.' Said to be prepared for a few weeks, but not to pack too much. Said we can buy what we need in the Territories. Didn't bother to tell me why, but there was an old soldier boy and a hard-looking man in buckskins sharing a coffee with Marshal Greer and Bowean."

Carson and his brothers dressed and swung onto their bareback horses. As they rode close to his parent's neat farmyard, his little brothers raced past.

As the younger boys raced into the yard, stirring a cloud of dust, Carson's mother stepped onto the porch, a pail of dirty dishwater in hand. At first, she smiled her biggest, warmest smile. "Back already?" Then her smile fled as she spotted Deputy Marty Dunnegan riding beside Carson.

Marty tipped his hat. "Nice to see you Mrs. Kettle."

Her lips smiled, but her eyes stayed somber as she nodded. "Deputy Dunnegan." She turned to Carson. "Already? You just got home."

Carson shrugged. "I guess this is what I signed up for."

*****

Marshal Greer sat behind his desk, playing cards fanned out in his hand. Deputy Marshal Gilmour Bowean sat across the desk, his thick right arm still strapped to his chest.

As Carson followed Marty through the door, the marshal looked up, folded his cards, and set them on the desk. "Found him, I see."

Dunnegan nodded and chuckled. "Weren't hard. Just talked to his pa, out working hard in the fields. Found Kettle here playing in the river with the children." He bumped Carson's shoulder and winked.

Carson's cheeks warmed. He started to explain that he'd rolled out of bed before the sun and fed the horses and the cattle and harnessed the mule and spent the morning plowing. And how after lunch, his father and mother had insisted he spend time with his younger brothers. Said the boys missed Carson so much when he was gone off marshaling..., and they all could use a few hours off.

Before he got all the words out, Marshal Greer said, "Pull up a chair, boys."

Once Carson and Marty had taken seats on either side of Bowean, Marshal Greer said. "I know you boys are green as grass, but everyone else is out in the Territories. I'd send Bowean here, but the doc says he's to stay here another week or two, and this can't wait."

Carson leaned forward. "What's happened?"

"Someone's killing Indians. Men, women, and children. We don't find them and stop them right now, we'll have a war on our hands. You boys pack light and leave first thing in the morning for Fort Sill."

"Fort Sill?" Carson asked. "It's all the way across the Territory. It must be a week's ride."

Marshal Greer nodded. "Five days if you push hard."

"What do we know?" Carson asked.

"Major Kinsey suspects someone's riding out of Greer County, Texas." He smiled. "No relation."

"Does the major know who? Or why?" Carson asked.

Marshal Greer shook his head. "That's all I know. That, and the army scouts haven't been able to track down the killers, and Major Kinsey sent two dispatch riders and asked for our help."

It shocked Carson that Marshal Greer would send him and Dunnegan, his two newest deputies, all the way past Fort Sill. "What can we do that the army scouts haven't already tried?"

Marshal Greer smiled and shook his head. "That was my thought, but it isn't often the army asks for our help, and when they do, I always say yes. Right now, you boys are all I've got. The dispatch riders are heading out at first light. Be ready to ride with them." He turned to Carson. "You're the senior man, Kettle, so you're in charge, but I don't want you taking any chances. Do what the Major asks, but I don't expect you two will find anything his scouts haven't found. You'll get mileage and expenses, but I doubt there will be any rewards."

Both Carson and Dunnegan sagged in their chairs.

The marshal continued. "Unless something changes, I expect to see you back here in three weeks or less. When you get back, I'll send you after an easy catch or two to make up for it."

*****

The cafe was still busy with the last of the dinner crowd. Carson crushed the crumbs of the flaky pie crust under his fork and swiped them across the last of the rich, sweet remnants of the apple pie filling on his plate.

Across the table Marty grinned and waved at the waitress as she hurried by. "That pie's awful fine, Nell. Think I could have another piece?"

Nell stopped mid-stride. "What about you, Deputy Kettle?" she asked with a shy grin.

Carson glanced up and met her smiling, dark eyes, then looked back at his plate. "I guess I'd better, Miss Brown. Sounds like it'll be a good long time before I get another as good."

She glanced over her shoulder and surveyed the diners remaining in the cafe. "Are you heading out into the Territories again?"

Carson nodded.

She held a hand over her heart. "It must be so exciting."

Carson's cheeks warmed. "Sometimes, but mostly it's long, hot days and cold nights on the hard ground."

Marty sighed, as if he'd heard it all before, and forced a smile. "Think we could get that pie?"

Nell blushed a pretty shade of pink and smiled at Carson. "Of course, Deputy Dunnegan. I'll fetch it right now."

Nell set the pie before them and refilled their coffee cups. She smiled at Carson. "They say you brought in Lijah Penne single handed and killed the gunman Jared Crusher."

"Nelly dear," an older woman sitting across the dining hall called. "I'll have a splash more coffee."

Nell blushed again and walked away.

Marty rocked his head left and right. "I hear you brought in that mean old Lijah Penne all by your lonesome, Deputy Kettle," he said in a high, falsetto voice.

Carson ignored him and cut off the point of his slice of pie with his fork.

"What's this?" Marty said, pointing from the sliver of pie on his plate to the wide wedge on Carson's.

Carson began to cut his slice down the middle. "Here. I'll give you some of mine."

Marty pressed his lips together and shook his head. "Don't bother. This is plenty for little ol' me."

*****

The next morning, well before dawn, Carson climbed out of his bed in the cells at the back of the Marshal's office. He had cleaned both his rifles and his pistol and filled his saddlebags with a clean shirt and a few provisions before turning in. Packed and ready to go, all he had to do was saddle his horse and ride.

Marty lay on his back on the cot in the next cell, snoring loudly, his mouth wide open.

Carson reached through the bars and shook him.

Marty snorted and rolled over. "What? What time is it? It's still dark."

"Won't be for long."

Marty rolled over and pulled the pillow over his head.

Carson pulled on his boots, picked up his rifles, saddlebags, bedroll, and slicker, and headed toward the livery.

As he slid back the heavy rolling door to the stable, Marty skidded to a stop beside him. "Why didn't you wait for me?"

Carson looked at his new partner and, without a word, marched toward his saddle, sitting on a rack at the back of the stable. Maybe Bowean wasn't such a terrible partner after all.

As the sun tickled the eastern horizon, they rode along the deserted main street of Fort Smith.

"What do you think of that Nell?" Marty asked.

"Seems like a nice girl."

"You sweet on her?"

Carson shook his head. "I barely know her."

"Seems like she's sweet on you."

"I doubt it. She doesn't know me any better than I know her."

"I'd like to take her for a walk when we get back."

Carson pressed his lips together and shook his head. "There they are."

In the pale light, two men, one in uniform and the other in fringed buckskins, sat outside the wooden gates set in the stone wall surrounding the garrison.

As they rode close, the uniformed sergeant turned and raised a hand. He wiped the back of his hand over his lips and swallowed the food he chewed. Even in the pale, dawn light, his ruddy cheeks glowed red in sharp contrast to the fringe of white hair showing under his hat. "You pilgrims the deputies?"

Carson nodded. "Yes, sir. I'm Deputy Kettle and this is Deputy Dunnegan."

"Y'all can just call me Marty," Marty said. "I've been just Marty my whole life."

The sergeant turned his horse, rode close, wiped his fingers on his trousers, and extended his hand. "Alf Buckley." He pointed to the man in buckskins. "And that friendly fellow is Gate Rudd."

Rudd's salt and pepper hair was tied in a tail that hung past his shoulders. He wore a wide-brimmed gray hat, tilted back over his long-sloped forehead.

Even when Carson rode close and held out his hand, Gate stared straight ahead. After a moment, Carson pulled back his hand and turned his horse back toward Marty and Alf.

Alf chuckled. "Don't mind Gate. He's a mighty good man on a trail, but he's not too happy about the Major sending us off on an eight-day jaunt to fetch you two."

Gate Rudd clucked to his horse, a leggy gray that looked like it could go all day and night. He started along the road southwest, keeping the Arkansas River to their right. As he passed Carson, he glanced over. "Try to keep up."1

CHAPTER two

Gate held to a grueling pace, never once turning back to see if his companions were keeping up. He stopped for two things: to allow his horse to drink from one of the many rocky streams that cut the road, or to survey the land ahead and around them.

Carson found himself wishing for the pace Bowean had set, an alternating of walking and trotting, 'to save the horses, in case we need them.'

By the time the sun reached its zenith, Carson's legs ached from the steady trotting. Sure, they had covered at least twenty miles, but he pushed his sorrel into a gentle lope, until the sorrel pulled alongside

Gate's gray. "We should rest these horses a spell," he said to the older man.

Gate grunted and flicked his head toward the sun. "Almost lunchtime." He turned his eyes back to the road and continued at the same pace.

Carson slowed his sorrel until Alf and Marty caught up. "He always keep a pace like this?"

Alf squeezed his lips together and nodded. "Most always."

Marty pointed ahead. "Look there."

A small village stood maybe three quarters of a mile further along the road.

Marty smiled. "Must be Scullyville. We should be able to get lunch there."

Alf chuckled. "I doubt it. I hope you packed something to eat."

Marty shrugged. "I've got bacon and beans and hardtack and jerky, but surely we'll stop if there's a cafe."

Alf smiled. "Get used to it. Gate won't stop in town unless he has to. He's a tad shy of people."

They trotted straight through town, weaving and dodging freight and farm wagons and people crossing the single street.

By the time they'd gone a mile past Scullyville, Carson's stomach rumbled.

Marty laughed. "Sounds like your belly thinks your throat's been cut."

Carson nodded.

Gate trotted through a clear little creek, then turned north. After a couple of hundred yards, he stopped under the canopy of a sprawling oak tree, beside the creek and at the edge of a grassy meadow. He pulled the saddle and bridle from his gray and turned him loose, with a slap on the hip. Then he dug into his saddlebags for an oilskin pouch, plopped down against the oak tree, pulled out a thick roast beef sandwich and a jar of buttermilk. Sergeant Alf pulled out the same, smacked his lips, and dug in.

Carson and Marty chewed on dry jerky and hardtack and sipped cool stream water from their canteens.

As soon as he'd finished his sandwich, Gate stood and wiped his hands on the dark, greasy thighs of his buckskins. He whistled, and the gray popped his head out of the grass and trotted to him.

The second day was more of the same. By late afternoon, Carson felt his strong sorrel flagging. No wonder Gate's horse looked like a greyhound.

"Look there," Marty said, pointing to a crudely lettered sign nailed to a dead tree. The sign read 'Perryville 10 Miles'. He turned to Alf. "Anything there?"

Alf nodded. "Big trading post and a stage station."

"Cafe?" Marty asked.

Alf again nodded.

"Hotel?"

Alf smiled. "Of sorts. But we won't be stopping."

Marty looked at Carson. "I say we stop. This horse of mine is about wore down. I bet we already done a hundred miles."

Carson nodded, then turned to Alf. "If you and Gate don't want to stop, you ride on. We can follow the road to Fort Sill, and we won't dawdle, but I won't kill a good horse to get there."

Alf grinned. "I guess we'll be stopping."

A mile on, they crossed a rough, rocky creek and crested the far bank. Three covered wagons stood off to one side of the road. The rear wheels of the lead wagon touched the box at the top, just below the tarp, and spread wide at the bottom, a broken axle. A tall salt-and-pepper-haired man, with a matching beard, hunched under the hooped tarp and handed a heavy wooden box from the wagon to two men waiting on the ground. Piles of crates and furniture stood beside the wagon on the roadside. A woman, dressed in a nondescript gray dress and matching big-brimmed sun bonnet, sat mending clothing in the shadow of a big old oak tree. A second similarly dressed woman laughed and ducked away from four little girls, ranging from maybe three to seven or eight years of age.

Gate slowed his horse, spoke to the men, tipped his hat, and rode by.

Carson slowed his horse, glanced at the disappearing scout, then turned to Alf. "I'm going to see if they need help."

Alf nodded and clucked to his horse. "I'll tell Gate to wait or come back. He won't like it, but the major told us to fetch you back with us and he's the one person Gate won't buck."

Carson and Marty pulled alongside the lead wagon, the one with the broken axle. "Can you use a hand?" Carson asked.

The man, about the age of Carson's father, poked his head out of the wagon. "I've got an extra axle here. Just have to dig it out. Your friend said you were in a big hurry, but we certainly could use a couple more strong backs, when the time comes to lift the wagon."

After tying their horses in the shade, Carson and Marty got in line and helped stack the last of the items from the wagon on the pile at the side of the road. Carson took the last crate and slumped at the weight of it. "Whoa! What's in here?"

"Books," the dark-haired man said. "I'm a teacher."

Gate Rudd stopped his horse beside the wagon. He snorted. "Wear those horses of yours out long before you get to Californy, carrying fooforaw like that."

The man leaned from the wagon and extended his hand toward Rudd. "Alessandro Foresti," he said. "Most call me Alex."

This time, Rudd extended his hand. "Gate Rudd."

Alex pointed to the other two men, one portly and about Alex's age, the other slim and closer to thirty. "These are my traveling companions. Frank Trajetta and Phillip Nolcini."

Alex smiled. "...and there are many things in this pile I would leave behind, before I left those books."

Rudd snorted again through his nose. "We best get that wagon up on blocks so we can all get on our way."

Alex jumped from the bed of the wagon, pulled a two-man saw from the edge of the pile, and held it against the wagon. He pulled a long belt knife and scratched the blade of the saw, a good foot from where the blade hit the bottom of the wagon bed, then he pointed to an ax leaning against a carton and turned toward a fallen tree fifty yards up the hill. "Come on Phillip. Let's cut a couple of blocks."

The dark-haired young man, sitting on the pile of boxes, pushed his palms against his knees and groaned as he stood. He twisted one corner of his long mustache. "Don't see how it's become my problem that you bought a broke down wagon."

Carson stepped forward. "Let Deputy Dunnegan and I cut the blocks. We been riding all day. Be good to get the kinks out of our backs."

Marty narrowed his eyes, but followed Alex and Carson up the hill.

Alex swung the axe, slashing at one of the limbs remaining on the downed tree.

After a few awkward strokes, Carson stepped forward. "Let me take a swing. Like I said, I've been sitting a horse all day and I need to stretch my back."

Alex handed Carson the axe.

Carson swung the axe like he knew what he was doing, and in fact, he did. While his father had been off fighting in the war, one of the day jobs Carson had taken to feed the family, had been helping their neighbor, old Mr. Gunther, clear a field of oak and hickory and prepare the logs for the barn, he then helped the old man build.

The axe needed a good sharpening, but even with that, Carson made quick work of the limbs. "Come on, Marty," he said, picking up the saw.

By the time they had sawed two blocks of equal length from the downed tree, sweat poured from both their brows. Alex reached for one of the blocks, but Carson said, "Take the saw. I'll get that." He turned to Marty. "Get the other one, Deputy."

Marty shook his head, as if he were about to complain, then he grinned and hoisted the heavy block onto his shoulder.

As they dropped the blocks behind the wagon, one of the women held out two cups of water. With barely a glance at the woman, who wore a loose gray dress and a large sun bonnet hiding her lowered face from his eyes, Carson took the cup, drained it, and handed it back. "Thank you, ma'am."

The woman raised her head. "It's miss."

Instead of the face of an older woman Carson had expected, he found himself staring into the most beautiful, dark brown eyes he had ever seen. "Thank... thank you... I thought..."

She grinned. "What did you think, Deputy?"

Carson shook his head, "Well, I expected something else."

"Bella," Alex said. "Get more water for the deputies, while we get this wagon up on these blocks, then get the children to gather some wood. The least we can do is feed these men for their help."

Gate stepped forward. "No need for that. We'll help you lift this wagon and be on our way."

Marty bumped Carson with his shoulder as they watched Bella walk toward the water barrel lashed to the side of the last wagon. Carson turned back toward Alex. "It is getting late. Our horses are tired. We'd be happy to join you for a meal."

Gate snorted through his nose but said nothing.

Marty pulled his eyes from the girl. "Yes.... Yes, we would."

Gate shook his head, but turned and grabbed the bottom edge of the wagon bed. Carson, Marty, and Alf joined him at the back of the wagon. Frank, the third man from the wagons, and Alex each took a corner.

Alex looked over his shoulder at Phillip. "Stand those blocks under the back edge once we lift it."

Phillip sighed and pushed himself up from his seat on the crate.

"On three," Alex said. "One. Two. Three."

The six men leaned back and strained.

"Higher," Phillip said from beneath the wagon.

The men struggled and strained.

"Higher!"

Carson pulled and lifted with all his strength.

"Okay," Phillip said. "Let it down easy."

The heavy wagon up on the blocks, Alex crawled under to undo the bolts holding the axle to the wagon frame. He struggled to loosen a heavy nut. His wrench slipped, and he slammed his knuckles into the broken axle. He winced and shook his hand, then pressed the torn, bleeding flesh to his lips.

Carson, watching with one hand resting on the wagon box, dropped to his knees and leaned under the wagon. "Let me help."

Alex's cheeks flushed through his dark, tanned skin. "I'm better with books."

Carson took the wrench and soon had the four nuts loosened from the brackets holding the axle to the bolster. While he worked, the others pulled the wheels from the broken axle.

In less than an hour, Carson re-tightened the nuts and crawled out from beneath the wagon. The smell of onions, garlic, pepper, and other spices, Carson didn't recognize, filled the air. His mouth watered and he licked his lips.

Bella looked up from the big pot she stirred and smiled.

Blood rushed to his face. But why? He knew nothing of the young woman. For all he knew, she was Phillip's betrothed. He lowered his eyes and turned to where Marty helped Alex lift one of the heavy, steel-shod wooden wheels onto the axle. As they slid it into place, Carson spun on the wheelnut, then wiped the axle grease from his hands on a clump of dry grass.

He turned to check on the fire and supper, and almost ran over Bella, standing behind him with a pot of warm water.

Her eyes sparkled bright, and glossy, dark hair framed her smiling face. She took a step back and set the steaming pot on the ground and handed him a bar of soap. "This should do a better job than that grass."

Carson's pulse quickened; Bella had removed her bonnet and exposed her beauty. He licked his lips. "I bet it will. Thank you."

She handed him the flour sack towel she had draped over one arm. "You're welcome."

Her hand brushed the back of his, stopping his breath.

She turned to the others. "Wash up. Supper's ready."

An hour later, Carson finished his second serving of stew. Not wanting to waste a single drop, he scraped the last of the rich, flavorful broth from his bowl.

Bella stepped close with the pot in her hands. "More?"

"No, thank you," Carson said. "But it was delicious. I'm guessing salt pork and canned tomatoes and onions, but there's a flavour I don't recognize. Almost a cross between sage and mint."

The fire flared and reflected in Bella's smiling eyes. "That's oregano. My grandma brought seeds on the boat when she came from Italy."

Carson licked the last of the soup from his spoon. "I like it a lot, Miss Foresti."

Bella touched his arm. "I'm glad, Deputy."

Still not comfortable with the title, Carson said, "You can call me Carson..., if you want to."

"All right, Carson. If you'll call me Bella."

Carson glanced toward the fire. To the left of the glowing coals, Marty looked up from the string game he played with the four little girls. He grinned and shook his head; to the right of the fire ring, Phillip twisted one side of his mustache, his staring eyes, narrow and cold.

CHAPTER three

Patricia Grimwald pinched her cheeks and brushed a stray lock of hair from her eyes. She ran her hands down the front of her lacey gown, smoothing away the wrinkles left from the long carriage ride. Riding a horse the thirty miles to Fort Sill would have been more like her and more comfortable. But she had a mission. And her fine dress and well-coiffed hair suited its aim much more than the men's trousers and tied-back hair she preferred.

She paced the room. Where was the major? His adjutant had said he'd be right in. She paused at the window. The adjutant stood near the gate of the white picket fence surrounding a little graveyard, fidgeting and wringing his hands. Through the pickets, the major's blue uniform showed as he knelt beside a white cross. Everyone knew his wife had died of fever during the winter, but surely he wasn't keeping her waiting for that. It had been months.

She turned from the window and pulled a book from the full wall of books lining one side of the office. 'On War' by Carl Von Clausewitz was a fitting title for a book owned by a military man. She opened a random page. *'If we read history with an open mind, we cannot fail to conclude that, among all the military virtues, the energetic conduct of war has always contributed most to glory and success.'*

She breathed in and thought of her father saying, 'no guts, no glory.' More or less the same thing.

The door opened, and Major Kinsey stepped into the room. Tall and trim, but with shoulders broad for a man of his stature and age, and a proud military bearing. And widowed. From a wealthy family and certainly worth consideration, but not today.

She smiled. "Major." Then she turned to re-shelve the book.

Major Kinsey smiled and stepped forward. "Miss Grimwald. So nice to see you." He held out a long-fingered hand. "What have you got there?"

She handed him the book.

He nodded. "An excellent book, but probably not to your taste." He strode to the far end of the bookshelf, squatted, and pulled a leather-bound book from a bottom shelf. "This may be more to the liking of a young woman such as yourself."

"Pride and Prejudice," she said as she took the book and glanced at the cover. "Doesn't seem like something a man like you would read," she said, grinning and meeting his eyes.

His smile fled, and he looked away. "It was my dear wife's."

Suddenly flustered, a condition she rarely found herself in, she lowered her eyes and held out the book. "I'm so sorry."

Major Kinsey took a deep breath, held out his hand to indicate she should hold on to the book, and forced a smile. "No apology needed. How could you know? Would you like to borrow it? You're most welcome to this one, or to any book that I have. I only ask that you return them."

She was about to refuse the books, then reconsidered. They would give her a reason to return anytime she needed more information. "May I take them both?"

The major smiled. "Certainly, though I'm not sure you'll get much enjoyment from the Von Clausewitz tome."

She returned his smile. "I find the art of war almost as fascinating as the men who wage it."

Now it was his turn to fidget. "Would you join me in a cup of tea?"

She liked strong, black coffee, preferably from a pot on the edge of a campfire, but she nodded. "I'd be delighted."

A few moments later, they sat in comfortable leather chairs near the window. The adjutant brought in a steaming teapot and two china cups on a silver tray.

As the dark tea cascaded into her cup, she caught an interesting hint of pine smoke.

The adjutant stood back as the major held his cup to his nose.

Patricia did the same. "It smells almost smoky."

The major set down his cup while the adjutant stirred in honey and poured in milk. "You're very perceptive. It's Lapsang Souchong. I'm told the Chinese smoke it over pine fires. My father purchases it from a Dutch trader in Boston and keeps me supplied. Try it with honey and milk. If it's not to your liking, Sergeant Haggen can bring you a pot of the tea the army serves the troops."

She nodded and set down her cup. The adjutant stirred in honey and milk, then turned and left.

Patricia raised her cup and sipped the sweet, smoky brew. Her eyes lit up. "I'm usually a coffee drinker, but this is delicious."

The major beamed. "I hoped you might like it. I'll send a pound home with you."

She shook her head. "You don't need to do that."

He leaned forward. "No, but I'd like to. Perhaps your father would like it."

"I'm sure he would."

"How is he?"

"Still struggling, but better. We got him a rolling invalid chair. He's learning to push himself around the house, but he hates the damn thing." She touched her fingers to her lips. "Excuse me. That's what he calls it."

The major chuckled. "No apology necessary."

She sipped her tea, then looked up. "We've heard rumors of trouble."

The major hesitated. "I suppose I can tell you." He set down his tea. "I don't know if there'll ever be peace. The land here's too fine. Hard enough to keep settlers out. Now, someone's killing Indians."

She lowered her eyes and remembered the breeze fluttering the red ribbons on the shirts of the five Keechi men, she and the boys had run down, killed, scalped, and hung by their necks from the limb of a huge oak tree. "What do you mean? I thought now the Indians had come into the Territories, that was all done."

He pursed his lips and nodded. "I thought so too. If it keeps up, there's sure to be an uprising. Not that they'd ever ask me, but I think the government needs to move the tribes further west and north. The Territories are just too fertile."

She raised one eyebrow.

"Don't get me wrong. I'll follow orders, but sometimes I think maybe it's time for me to get out. Right now, it's all I can do to push the settlers on west and to convince the chiefs to keep their young men in the fields. I've been meaning to ride out and talk to your father. It might be better if you came and stayed at the Fort until this trouble blows over."

"He'd never leave our house and horses, especially not if the savages were on the warpath. And he's got a thousand head of young cows coming up from down south."

"A thousand head?"

She nodded.

"I figured Warren wouldn't come in, but I thought maybe with his injury."

She shook her head.

"Might still be wise if you stayed here..., or came back."

She leaned forward and touched his wrist. "As pleasant as that might be, I'll stand with the old man. He raised me to be the son he never had, and that's what I'll be."

The major nodded. "Oh my. You could never be a son." He caught himself and cleared his throat. "If you change your mind, we'd be happy to house you, all of you, here."

"That's kind of you."

"If you catch wind of who might be doing this, would you send word?"

"Of course," she said, knowing that she wouldn't.

CHAPTER four

After supper, Carson wandered out to stretch his legs and check on his horse. As he passed a big hickory, a flash of movement caught his eye. He jerked and touched his pistol. When Gate chuckled, Carson relaxed and took a breath.

"Scare ya, boy?" Gate asked.

"I didn't see you there."

"Lucky I weren't a Comanche on the prod. I'd be wearing your hair. And more'n likely, I'd already be gone with your pony too."

"Good thing that's mostly done," Carson said.

Gate smiled for the first time since Carson had met him. "Don't seem likely the peace will last. Not with the killing that's been going on."

"Who do you think's doing it?" Carson asked. "And why?"

Any hint of humor left Gate's face. "Can't say who, but those of us seen what the savages can do, don't have to look far for a reason."

"Hopefully, we can find out who's doing it and stave off a war."

Gate smiled again. "You want to stop a war, you'd best get some shuteye. Then come back here at midnight and watch these horses. We leave at first light, and I don't want to walk. Sooner we get you to Fort Sill, sooner you can get home to your momma."

Carson sucked in a deep breath. "What's your problem with us?"

"No problem, boy," Gate said, then he pulled his hat over his eyes and leaned back against the tree.

Carson stood a minute, then turned and marched out toward the grazing horses.

The sorrel, shining almost golden in the bright moonlight, stood with the other saddle horses and a little apart from the heavy gray horses belonging to Mr. Foresti and the others.

Satisfied the horses were safe, he turned and cut through the trees and toward the creek. When he could, he liked to wash the sweat, salt, and smoke from his neck and face before climbing into his bedroll.

He ambled along, mired in his thoughts. Why was someone killing Indians? Was it as Gate seemed to think, nothing more than revenge for past savagery? Why now? Why here?

A flash of movement caught his eye through the trees. His heart jumped. This time, instead of going for his gun, he ducked behind a clump of sweetshrub.

Bella knelt, her bare back to him, one hand in the creek, rinsing her head and flowing black hair under a three-foot-high waterfall.

His heart raced. What would she think of him? Would she think he was sneaking around? Should he just creep away? Pretend it never happened? What if she saw him? He peeked around the shrubs.

Her back now straight, she squeezed the water from her hair.

He turned away, but the gentle curve of her back in the moonlight stuck in his mind's eye. He started back the way he'd come, then he turned and again ducked behind the sweetshrub. "Bella," he said in a voice just above a whisper. Nothing. He cleared his throat. "Bella."

She gasped. "Who's there?"

"It's me, Carson."

"Go away! What are you doing?"

"I'm sorry. I just came from the horses. I was going to wash up, myself. I didn't know you were here."

"I can't see you."

"Are you covered?"

"I'm covered."

He stepped from behind the shrubs. She had slipped on her chemise and held a towel in front of her chest. He shuffled out into the open. "I'm so sorry. I would have just left, but I didn't want you to think I was spying on you."

She smiled. "Weren't you?"

His face burned. "I... I guess I was, but I didn't mean to."

"Let me put on my blouse, then come over here."

He turned away, waited, and listened for the sound of anyone else approaching.

"Come here, quick," she said. "Before someone comes."

Not sure what to do, he did as she asked.

As he drew near her, he bowed his head and wrung his hat in his hands.

She stepped forward and lifted his chin. "I believe you."

He swallowed. "Thank you, and I am sorry. I'd best be going."

Her eyes twinkled as she held out a bar of soap. "You might want this if you're going to wash."

Again, he felt his cheeks warm. "I usually just rinse a bit."

"Take it," she said, thrusting the soap toward him. "You'll smell better."

He started to speak, but she touched his lips with one finger. "I'm teasing." She took his hand and placed the slick bar of soap against his palm.

A flowery smell hit him. Lavender?

"I'd better get back," she said.

He nodded.

She took a step away, then turned, stepped against him, and kissed his cheek.

"What was that for?"

"For helping us with the wagon and, well, for..." She turned and was gone.

He touched his cheek and wandered to the edge of the creek. Waves of desire coursed up and down his body. He pushed them away. He had a job to do. He didn't even know her. What did she stop herself from saying?

While he washed the sweat and smoke from his body, visions filled his head. How she'd seen after the younger children. Taken care of the cooking. Her easy smile as she did it all, without once being told or even asked.

He rinsed the bar of soap and set it on a flat rock, then sat back on his heels to allow the air to dry him. He picked up his shirt and wished he'd brought out the clean one from his saddlebags. His Deputy Marshal badge thudded against his chest.

He didn't even know her, and he had a job to do.

CHAPTER five

As the sun pushed a crescent of pink light over the treetops to the east, Carson stood, lifted his hands over his head, and stretched his back. Between the grueling pace Gate had held them to the day before and the sawing and lifting, waves of pleasure coursed through him, as the kinks in his tight, young muscles burned, then fell away. He rubbed his eyes, then touched a spot on his cheek. If things were different..., maybe.

At the sound of footsteps, he reached around and picked up his rifle.

Gate marched out from where he'd slept apart from the others. "Catch your horse. Might as well catch your partner's too. Time to get moving."

Something snapped inside Carson. "You go on then. Deputy Dunnegan and I can find Fort Sill, just fine by ourselves."

Gate puffed up, as if about to argue, then he brushed by and whistled. His horse lifted his head, then trotted toward them. "When would the deputies like to leave?" Gate asked.

"As soon as we've had a cup of coffee and maybe some breakfast."

Gate shook his head and slid the bridle on the gray.

Carson left his and Marty's horses to graze. With the pace they had traveled, and would likely travel again, the horses could use all the grass they could get.

He walked past Marty, still deep in his bedroll, and nudged him with his boot. "Time to get up."

He smelled biscuits before he saw Bella bent over a stump, slicing bacon. He looked left and right, then pulled the bar of soap from his pocket. "This must be yours. I found it by the creek."

She smiled. "Good morning Deputy. You keep that soap. The people you arrest will appreciate it."

"We're going to have a quick breakfast and hit the trail."

"Breakfast will be a few more minutes," she said.

"We've got biscuits. But I would take a cup of that coffee."

"Cold biscuits?" she asked. "When I went to all the trouble, to bake these fresh for you?"

His cheeks warmed. "It's not that. It's just that Gate..."

The corner of her sparkling eyes crinkled. "Mr. Gate Rudd can wait for breakfast too. It will only be a few minutes."

A hand clapped Carson on the shoulder. His heart jumped.

Bella's father, Mr. Foresti, laughed. "I guess you've been told. I'm going to see to our horses."

Carson helped himself to a cup of rich, strong coffee and leaned against the wagon.

Slices of smoky bacon sizzled as Bella slid them one-by-one into the big frying pan. She lifted the front of her skirt, squatted, and waved a hand over the Dutch oven sitting on a bed of coals at the edge of the fire. She pulled a flour sack towel from her shoulder and tossed it at Carson. With a laugh in her voice, she said, "Make yourself useful and set those biscuits on that stump. They're done."

Phillip trudged up from his wagon, rubbing his eyes. Without saying a word, he took the towel from Carson, lifted the lid from the Dutch oven, and reached inside.

"Leave those for these men," Bella said. "I'll make us another batch once they're on the road."

Phillip straightened his back and glared, then bent over and reached back into the oven.

"Phillip!" Bella said. "I said wait. Take your children to the creek and get them washed."

Phillip narrowed his eyes. Then turned and started back to his wagon, mumbling. "Once you're my wife, you won't be bossing me around like this."

Carson's cheeks burned, and he turned to see if Marty was coming.

Bella touched his wrist and motioned toward his cup with the coffeepot she held. "Don't worry about him. He lost his wife, and he's got big ideas about me, but I've got plans of my own and they don't include him, as much as I love his children."

Carson held out his cup. "What are your plans?"

She looked down. "First, I want to get my father settled in California, then I want to write about our adventures." She met his eyes. "Those plans aren't cast in stone. What are your plans, Deputy Kettle?"

Marty stomped up with his cup in hand. "I'll take a cup of that Arbuckles, if you please."

Bella filled his cup, then set the pot on the coals and turned the bacon.

Marty bumped Carson with his shoulder. "What'd I interrupt?"

Carson shook his head. "Nothing."

Marty grinned and nodded. "Nothing."

Sergeant Alf led his horse up and tied it to the wagon wheel. "You boys best eat a good breakfast. The mood Gate's in, there won't be much stopping today."

"Bring your plates, gentlemen," Bella said. "Breakfast is served." She looked around. "Where's Mr. Rudd?"

Alf held out his plate and chuckled. "He don't eat much. Get's by on less than any man I know, but you can give me his share."

A half hour later, Carson wiped his plate clean with a clump of grass.

Bella handed him a warm, paper-wrapped bundle of biscuit and bacon sandwiches.

"You don't need to do that," he said.

"I want to."

He took the food. "Thank you."

She touched his hand. "Thank you..., for helping my father. Will I see you again, Deputy Kettle?"

Her warm hand on his seemed to sweep the words from his mouth. "I... We... We'll be at Fort Sill, or thereabout. Maybe when you come through."

"I'll look forward to it," she said with a smile.

Marty walked up. "We'd best not keep old Gate waiting any longer."

Carson nodded. "I'll be right there." He turned back to Bella. "There's been trouble ahead. Keep that shotgun handy."

She squeezed his hand. "You be safe too."

*****

Alf was right. Other than stopping to water the horses and let them blow at the top of long hills, Gate held them to a blistering pace. Midday came and went. Carson turned in his saddle and pulled out the sandwiches Bella had packed for them. He rode the sorrel close to Marty and Alf and gave them each a bacon-filled biscuit, then he pushed up beside Gate. When the tall man looked over, he held out a biscuit.

Gate glanced his way. "I got jerky. Man can go a long way on jerky and water."

Carson extended the sandwich. "Go a long way on soft biscuits and smoky bacon too."

The corners of Gate's mouth and eyes lifted very slightly. Without slowing his horse, he took the sandwich, nodded, and turned his eyes back to the trail ahead. "Won't have to stop for supper now."

An hour further along the trail, they topped a rise. Buzzards and crows flapped and squawked into the air. The smell of death drifted on the breeze. A two-wheeled cart lay toppled, one wheel in the air. Bags of beans spilled onto the roadside. The horse or mule that had pulled the cart was gone, but the man, who had driven it, and what looked to be his wife and three children, lay scattered on the bloody ground.

Gate reined up his gray. "Mexicans."

As he pulled his sorrel to a stop, Carson took in the clothing and the bloody heads. He choked back his lunch. "Indians?"

Gate shook his head.

"But they're all scalped."

"No ears," Gate said.

Carson glanced from Gate to Alf and Marty.

Alf nodded. "Someone's paying bounty."

Carson raised one eyebrow.

"Those that pay make them bring both ears on the scalp, so they don't try to get paid more than once for the same kill."

Marty stepped off his horse. "Bounty on Mexicans?"

Alf stepped down beside him. "Hard to tell one black-haired scalp from the next, though this is what's got the Indians stirred up as well. This is why the major sent us after you, though I figure he wanted Bowean."

Carson puffed up. Why did everyone think Bowean was so much? Then Bella's long dark mane, as she bathed in the moonlight, flashed across his mind. He spun the sorrel, then he stopped, stepped off and turned to Alf. "Give me your shovel. We'll bury these folks, then go after whoever did this. Look around. See if you can find their tracks."

Gate rode up. "Judging by the smell, this happened yesterday, or even before. Whoever did it'll be long gone. We've tried to track 'em before. After a mile or so, they scatter, but maybe today will be different. Let's ride." He turned his horse.

Carson looked up, unbelieving. "We can't just leave them."

Gate looked over his shoulder. "Worms or buzzards. End result's the same. Even the Good Book says dust to dust. Move them off the road and let's ride."

Carson stepped close to Alf's horse and untied the short shovel the soldier carried to dig latrine pits and holes in the sod for fires. "It won't take long if we all take turns."

Gate mumbled something about pilgrims, then stepped off his gray, unsaddled him, pulled off the bridle, and turned the big horse loose. He grabbed the shovel and thrust it into the soft dirt at the side of the road.

Within an hour, with all of them taking turns, they had two holes, maybe four feet deep. They rolled the man and one of the children into one hole and the woman and the other two children into the other.

Carson wiped the sweat from his brow. "Anybody know some words to say over them?"

The other three men all looked away.

Carson cleared his throat. "Lord. We don't know these people, but they look to be simple farmers, killed for no good reason. Look after them and help us find those that did this and those that are paying bounties for scalps." He hesitated and took a deep breath. "And protect our new friends back along the trail." He picked up the shovel and began tossing dirt into the first hole.

The graves filled, Carson looked up. About fifty yards along the road, Gate sat his gray. When he saw Carson looking, he pointed south into the trees. "Five of them. Come on, if you're coming."

They followed Gate, who followed the tracks for about a mile, until he stopped and pointed east. "Same thing. First one cut off here."

"Let's follow the group," Carson said.

"Won't do no good," Gate said, but he turned his horse back south.

Ten minutes later, another set of tracks turned off from the group. "Seen enough?" Gate asked.

"Let's keep going."

Gate spit on the ground and started his horse. At the point where the next horse had turned from the group, he stopped again.

Carson rode up close. "They have to come back together sometime, and they have to go somewhere to get paid for the scalps. I say we go on."

Gate looked from Carson to Alf. "Tell him."

Alf cleared his throat. "We done this before. These boys are cagey. I'm afraid we're wasting our time."

Marty said, "Maybe we should split up."

Gate shook his head. "I told the major I'd bring you to the fort. I won't have you traipsing off getting killed."

Marty looked from Gate to Carson.

Carson shrugged his shoulders, then rode past the other three and continued to follow the tracks of the remaining two killers. He followed until they split, then without stopping, continued following the trail that continued south. After half an hour, the tracks led into a boggy creek, but failed to come out the other side. He hesitated, then turned to Marty. "Take the other side. He has to leave the creek sometime."

"How do we know which way he went?" Marty asked.

"We don't," Carson said. He turned to Alf. "Why don't you two go the other way?"

Gate rode up. "Nope, we stick together."

After fighting the thick brush along the creek for more than an hour, the hot afternoon began to cool as the sun sank lower and lower. Carson was about to give up, when he spotted a freshly broken branch and, below it, horse tracks. "I knew it," he said. "Come on back over, Marty."

They followed the single set of tracks northeast. Soon the sign showed all the outlaws' horses had come back together. Carson said nothing, but pride filled his chest. How could somebody like Gate, a renowned scout and tracker, have not already found these men? He turned the sorrel onto the well-traveled trail and kicked him into a trot.

In a small clearing, they found trampled grass where the horses had been picketed and the remains of a small, cold, but not old, campfire.

They continued on. After another half hour, Carson's heart sank. A dog barked and buzzards rose and fell and circled above and beyond the next hill. He paused the sorrel and pointed to the sky, then turned to ride over the hill.

Gate stopped beside him and grabbed the sorrel's rein. "Don't go charging in. They could still be about."

They stopped before the crest of the hill. Leaving Marty and Alf to watch their backtrail, Gate and Carson crept forward. Below, six dirt and stick huts sat in a large clearing. A skinny yellow dog, foam streaming from his jowls, tore around, charging at any crow or buzzard that tried to land on one of the many scalped, earless bodies scattered around the clearing.

Carson's eyes scanned for signs the killers were still about. Then he rose to his feet.

Gate whispered, "Look to be Cherokee. Let's make sure the tracks lead away before we get out in the open. "

Carson nodded.

Staying to the trees, they circled the encampment, until they cut the killers' tracks heading back toward the road to Fort Sill, they themselves had left hours before.

Carson looked at the bodies scattered around the village. The light was fading fast. He started the sorrel at a fast trot along the trail the killers had taken.

Marty had to lope his horse to catch up. "Where you going? What about those bodies?"

Carson glanced over and said four words. "Bella and the others."

CHAPTER six

Patricia and three riders followed Cashe Creek south. After a half-hour, bouncing along in the buggy on the rough two-track trail they followed, she pulled up the team of matched bays. She turned toward the youngest of the three heavily armed men that rode with her. "I've had enough of this contraption. Your turn to drive Gill."

The young man frowned, but squeezed his lips together and stepped from his horse.

Patricia hopped from the carriage. "You boys look away," she said as she dropped her hat behind the seat and unbuttoned the front of her dress. She pulled the dress over her head, slipped out of her petticoats and into a pair of well-worn men's trousers and a soft, blue linen shirt. She pulled a gun belt from beneath the wagon seat and buckled it around her waist. Then she pulled out the .36 caliber Colt Navy, checked the five loads, rested the hammer on an empty chamber, and re-holstered.

By the time she was ready, Gill had shortened the stirrups and stood holding the dun cow pony. He handed her the reins and grumbled under his breath as he climbed onto the carriage.

She scratched the pony's neck, mounted, and sighed. "That's better."

As they rode along, she pointed at the hill to the west. A gentle breeze stirred through the stirrup-high bluestem and other grasses. "Look at all that feed, Uncle Cliff, and not a cow on it."

The oldest of the men riding beside her nodded. "Won't be long now, Miss Patty."

The corners of her mouth rose, and her eyes wandered over the rolling hills. She nodded. "Won't be long." She turned and looked at the weathered old man, his once black hat, now gray from rain and sun and dust, and his cheeks deeply lined from exposure to the same elements. "What do you think of the major, Uncle Cliff?"

The old man cocked his head and grinned. "He cuts a fine figure, but he's not our kind. He's a man more likely to follow a trail already mapped, than to cut his own."

She raised her eyebrows and scratched her chin. "He does look good in that uniform..., and he seems lonely. I wonder if I could bring him around to our way of thinking?"

The old man chuckled. "If anyone could, it'd be you." He sat up straight and pointed south. "Look there." Down the long slope, across the Red River and many miles to the south, a cloud of red-tinged dust floated above the horizon. "Must be your daddy's cows."

Patricia whooped and spurred the dun down the slope at a run. Without even slowing, she drove the horse into the Red River in a cascade of muddy water. She pushed the gelding across the gravel bottom and into the deeper channel, where he had to swim a few strides, before reaching the shallow water on the south side, the Texas side. The land where a man, or a woman, could make her fortune, but a land filling up with settlers and sodbusters.

While she waited for the others to catch up, the dun shook like a dog. She laughed as he shimmied her back and forth.

As Cliff rode out of the river, she shouted. "Come on, old man. Let's go tell Daddy. Maybe this'll get him out of his mood."

As they galloped up to the big white clapboard ranch house, the three big-headed curs guarding the place dashed out, barking and wagging their tails. Patricia leaped from her horse, and without stopping to give the dogs their usual scratches, bounded up the stairs and into the house. "Daddy! Daddy!" She hesitated. Her heart stopped as she waited and listened for a reply. "Daddy? Where are you?"

Wooden wheels bumped over the polished plank floor as her father wheeled himself from the kitchen into the parlor. "What's got into you? There's no need to shout. I'm still here. Haven't done myself in, yet."

"Oh, Daddy don't say that. The cattle are coming."

For a second, he sat a little straighter. "Today?"

She grinned and nodded. "Appears so. There's a big cloud of dust down south."

He slumped back into his chair. "We're not ready. We need that grass."

She rushed to the back of his chair and pushed him toward the door. "Never mind that right now. Soon as Gill gets here with the carriage, we're going to go meet the herd."

An hour later, Patricia and her father bounced over the prairie. She held the reins in her hands while he pressed one hand to the side of the seat and struggled to hold himself upright.

"Slow down," he said. "Before you toss me out of this thing."

She eased back on the reins. "Sorry Daddy. I'm just so excited."

He pushed down with both powerful arms and scooted himself more fully on the seat. "To see the cows, or Britt?"

She looked at him from the corner of her eye. "Not Britt. Why would you say that?"

"I see the way he looks at you. You could do worse. He knows cattle and horses, and guns, and I won't always be around to look after you."

"Don't say that. Besides, I can look after myself."

"From what I hear, the other girls fancy him."

She laughed. "What girls? The whores in Eagle Springs?"

He shook his head. "Listen to you talk. I wish your mother was here to tell you these things, but it's just like a stud horse, a man's got needs, and you can't fault the horse or the man for that."

She chuckled and turned to look at the old man, but his face had turned stony, and he stared down into his lap.

"What do you think of Major Kinsey?"

He looked up. "Kinsey? Not our kind."

"He runs a tight ship at the Fort. Maybe I could win him over to our side."

Her father shook his head. "Where do you get these notions? Kinsey will never be like us. From all I can see, he's an Indian lover. He'd never do what has to be done. And besides, he's a Yankee."

"I think you might be misjudging him. He's had about all he can stand of looking after savages and keeping settlers at bay."

"He say anything about the savages getting killed?"

She licked her lips and grinned. "Asked me to let him know if I got any word about who was doing it." She glanced at her father, hoping to see him smile, but his face was dull and ashen, and he had dropped his eyes back to his lap.

They topped a small rise. A thousand head of cattle trudged north and stretched south, maybe ten head wide and a hundred head deep. Red dust boiled from the dry ground as the hooves of 960 cows and calves and forty thick-necked, muscular bulls cut into the sod.

"Just look at them, Daddy," Patricia said as she turned the carriage west. "Once we get them settled, we'll start culling those bulls and bring in some English stock. Before you know it, you'll be bigger than Captain King."

For the first time that day, the old man smiled. He held the side of the wagon seat with his right hand and squeezed Patricia's forearm with his left. "Maybe so."

Warmth flooded her chest.

The wagon bumped over a big, round rock and bounced their bottoms off the seat. The wheelchair clattered in the wagon bed, and the old man's smile fled. "Best you watch where we're going. Be a long ride back to the house, in that chair, you break a wheel."

A tall, blonde cowboy galloped toward them on a leggy buckskin and white pinto, with a yellow-streaked black mane. Broad of shoulder and slim of waist, he cut a fine figure, even covered in trail dust, and sporting a week's growth of whiskers.

He jerked the pinto to a sliding stop, sending red dust over Patricia and her father. He touched the brim of his hat. "Boss. Miss Patty. What do you think?"

Patricia frowned. "I think you should be a little more careful with that horse, Britt Viola. You could break his leg, jerking him into this rocky ground like that."

Britt grinned. "Ain't broke him yet. He's tough. But I mean the cows."

She shook her head. "I know what you mean." Her face softened. "They look fine." She broke into a grin and touched her father's arm. "They look wonderful."

Her father nodded. "Any trouble?"

Britt grinned. "Nothing we couldn't handle. Ran into some old boys who figured we should pay to cross some old creek they claimed was theirs."

The old man shook his head. "How much did they want?"

"Ten cents a head."

"Hope you didn't pay them."

Britt grinned and patted his Colt. "We added seven horses to the remuda."

"Any of our boys hurt?" Patricia asked.

"Remy's got a boil on his backside. Hard for him to ride."

She shook her head. "I mean by the herd cutters."

Britt shook his head. "Horace seen 'em sneak around long before we got there, so we done a little sneaking of our own. Next thing they know'd they was buzzard meat." He turned from Patricia to her father. "How's things going here?"

The old man shook his head. "The boys are out doing their job, but we haven't got the war we need yet. We're gonna have to stir the nest even more I'm afraid."

Britt frowned, scratched at the scab through and above his right eyebrow, then smiled. "Soon as we get these critters settled, I'll take Horace and Remy and we'll sure enough stir things up."

Patricia caressed the bone grips on her Colt. "Let's get these cows home."

CHAPTER seven

Branches, like bony fingers, clutched and tore at Carson's hat and shirtsleeves as he drove the sorrel along the overgrown trail the killers had recently followed, but he ducked his head and kept his eyes on the torn-up soil of the trail. He coughed and spat sour, bitter bile from his throat. Fear and urgency coursed up and down his spine. The only thing he heard was the thunder of the sorrel's hooves on the trail and the scrape and crack of branches against his clothes.

Only when he broke from the trees and onto the road did he stop. He leaped from his horse, squatted, and struggled to make out the tracks in the dim light.

He stood and pulled a match from his saddlebag and lit it with his thumbnail.

The others crashed into the road, and their horses slid to a stop to avoid smashing into the sorrel.

Carson shook out the match, swung onto the sorrel, pushed him through and past the others, leaned over his big horse's neck, and galloped east down the road.

After two miles, the sorrel slowed. Gate, leaning forward, pushed his leggy gray up to Carson's side. "Slow down, or you'll kill that pony."

Carson sat up and let the sorrel coast along. "They can't be that far ahead."

Boom! Boom, boom! Three shots rang out from east along the road.

Carson lashed the sorrel with the end of his reins and leaned back over his neck. The big horse dug in and took off at a run.

They topped a rise, and a half mile ahead, the three covered wagons, belonging to Bella's family and friends, stood in the middle of the road. The big gray draft horses looked up from where they stood, still harnessed to the three wagons.

Carson's eyes darted left and right as he rode toward the wagons. He jerked out his pistol. A woman's body, her full gray dress splayed out around her, lay sprawled at the side of the road. His breath left him, but he stayed on his horse until Gate rode up beside him. "Keep watch," he said, as he leaped from the sorrel.

It was Frank's wife, Mrs. Trajetta, most of her graying hair and both ears skinned from her bloody skull.

Carson gagged as he snatched up the bonnet laying near her and set it over her head before dropping his reins and sprinting to the first wagon. He pressed his head inside the canvas covering. "Bella?" he shouted.

The next earless, scalpless body belonged to Bella's father, Alex. Carson stood and glanced around as the others galloped up from the west.

Another scalped body lay in the road near the second wagon. Frank. Carson left him and ran and thrust his head into the third wagon. No one there. Where were Bella, the children, and Phillip?

He crashed into the brush along the trail. "Bella! Phillip?" He spun one way and then the other. "Bella!"

Marty threw his arms around him. "Stop. It's too dark. You'll stomp all over their tracks. Let's find a lantern."

Carson threw up his arms and shrugged Marty away, started forward, then he dropped his face into his hands. "Who would do something like this? Why?" After a moment, he stood tall, took a deep breath, and turned to the nearest wagon. "You're right. Let's find a lantern."

He lit a match, leaned into the back of Phillip's wagon, found a lantern wedged into the corner of the wagon box, pulled it out, then paused and listened. He held his breath.

Marty stepped close. "Give me the lantern."

"Hush!" Carson said. "Listen."

"Bella? Phillip?" Carson shouted as he broke from the wagon and into the brush.

Marty lit the lamp and followed.

Carson crept forward, his pistol drawn and cocked. Every few strides, he stopped. "I heard something. I swear it." He motioned to Marty. "Bring the lantern up here."

Marty held the lantern high. Bella's father's shotgun lay on the ground.

"Bella?" Carson said.

A tiny voice squeaked from the undergrowth. "Deputy Marty?"

Marty spun and pointed the lantern into the undergrowth. "Gemma?"

"Pappa's hurt," Gemma said.

Marty left Carson. "Where are you? Are your sisters there?"

"Are the wicked men gone?"

"They are," Marty said.

The oldest of Phillip's daughters stood and showed herself. "We're all here, but Pappa's hurt."

Carson bumped past Marty. "Where's Bella?"

Gemma looked down. "Gone."

"What do you mean?"

"Pappa shot at them, but they took her."

Carson turned and grabbed the handle of the lantern.

Marty jerked it back. "Let go."

Carson moved to again grab the lantern, but Alf threw his arms around him. "Stop! It's too dark to go running off half-cocked."

Marty stepped close to Gemma. "Where's your pappa and your sisters?"

"Back here. They shot Pappa and he won't wake up."

Carson struggled to free himself from Alf's grasp. "Let me go. Y'all take care here. I'm going after them."

Gate stepped in front of Carson and looked at Alf. "If the high and mighty U.S. Deputy Marshal wants to get his fool head shot off and the girl killed, let him go do it."

Carson stopped struggling. Gate and Marty were right. It was too dark to go after Bella, and he was a Deputy U.S. Marshal, and Marshal Greer had put him in charge. He took a deep breath. "I'm all right." He turned to Marty. "Take care of the girls and their pa. I'll just wander a bit further along and ..."

Marty nodded. "Don't go too far."

An hour later, Phillip sat near a small fire, his four daughters around him, and a bandage around his head.

Phillip had no memory of what happened, but Gemma told them he sent Bella to hide with the children while he held off the bad men. After he shot one man off his horse, and the men shot him, Bella made a dash for the shotgun, but before she could get it, another of the men grabbed her by the hair and dragged her away through the trees.

Carson took a lantern. The stench of blood and an unwashed, stinking body, led him to a spot not far off the trail the killers had taken, where a tall, thin, filthy man sprawled in the brush. Phillip's shotgun blast had removed a two-inch chunk of skull and brain from above his right ear.

Carson set the lantern on the ground, knelt beside the body, and checked the pockets.

He jumped when Gate stepped in behind him and said, "Shine that lantern on his face. He looks familiar."

Carson lifted the lamp.

"Don't know his name but I've seen him and some other buffalo skinners at the Fort."

Carson looked up. "I don't understand. What's going on here?"

Gate shook his head. "The major thinks maybe someone's gone crazy with grief and is taking revenge."

Carson waited for more. "What do you think?"

"Someone's paying for the scalps."

"Why?"

"Could be revenge," Gate said.

"Revenge?" Carson asked. "Revenge for what? Surely these folks haven't done anything to deserve this. And what about the Mexican family, and the Cherokees? What's the link?"

"Like Alf told you, black hair. Hard for someone paying to tell one black-haired scalp from another. 'Specially if they was dumped outta the same sack."

Carson grabbed the dead man's shirt and shook the body. "What kind of man were you to do something like this to these good people?" He slammed a fist into the dead man's stiff, cold ribs.

Gate touched his shoulder. "Leave him for the coyotes. We'll go after the girl at first light."

Carson looked up. "Why didn't they just kill her and take her scalp?"

Gate dropped his eyes and turned away.

Carson bounced to his feet and ran toward the fire. "What time was it when the wicked men came?"

Gemma looked up. "We were looking for a place to stop for the night."

Phillip nodded. "I do remember that."

Carson turned to Marty. "Find some oil for this lantern. I'll get our horses."

Marty stayed seated. "It's too dark. We use the lantern to track them, they'll see us coming from a mile away. Let's wait till first light."

Alf nodded. "He's right."

Carson glanced at the children, paused, and said, "I won't leave her with them, one second longer than I have to."

Phillip met Carson's eyes, then turned to the other men and pushed himself up onto his shaking feet. "You watch my girls. I'll go with him. Give me a horse."

"Pappa. No!" Gemma shouted. She grabbed his sleeve with one hand and Marty's with the other. "Can't you go, Deputy Marty?"

"Come on, Marty," Carson said as he strode away from the fire and toward the horses.

Gate pushed forward. "I'll come."

An hour later, Carson led the sorrel through the trees. The killers had not tried to hide their tracks, but the dark shadows still made tracking difficult.

Two hours later, his feet ached, and his eyes burned from lack of sleep and overuse. The trees thinned, and the moon peeked through and lit up the ground. Carson mounted and held up the lantern. "Between this and the moon, I can see enough from up here now. Let's go. They have to stop sometime."

They rode to the edge of the trees and stopped before riding onto a wide expanse of grassland. On the far side of the grassy flat, maybe two miles distant, light flickered on trees. A fire?

Carson held up the lamp, then quickly lowered it and turned down the wick until the flame went out. "It has to be them," he whispered. He burned to kick the sorrel into a gallop, but instead, he turned and skirted the trees. "Let's see if we can get around them."

"They've already seen us," Gate said.

"What?"

Gate pointed across the grassland. The firelight no longer flickered off the leaves.

Carson turned the sorrel south along the edge of the trees and pushed him into a dangerous nighttime gallop.

CHAPTER eight

The firelight danced through the fabric of Bella's dress, which had been pulled up and covered her eyes. Part of her burned to shake her head free and suck in a breath of fresh air, but a stronger, deeper, more stubborn part stopped her. Though she longed to see..., to forever mark into her memory the faces of the beasts who'd killed her father and her friends and.... Another part of her wanted to stay hidden. Pretend none of this had ever happened.

She twisted her hands; the coarse rope, lashing them against the rough oak bark, bit into her tender wrists, but she felt no slack. Somehow, despite what had happened, despite her pain and her loss, she had to find a way to get free. Phillip's little girls, the girls she loved with all her heart, were alone.

She eased her heels into the dirt and, ever so slowly, pushed, hoping to put some slack in the rope. Her bare backside slid across the rough ground. She fought back a sob. No matter what they'd done to her, or taken from her, she had to get back to the girls.

Not far away, the four animals who had killed her loved ones and savagely used her, laughed and drank.

"You boys take her legs. I'm gonna have another go before bed." It was the voice of the huge, foul-smelling man who had caught hold of her before she could reach the shotgun. If only she'd been a second faster, he'd be dead.

Raucous laughter filled the night.

She drew her legs tight against herself.

One of the other men let out a high-pitched giggle. "Still got a little fight. You was right to keep her alive, Yost."

Yost, the big man who had grabbed her, laughed. "Ain't I always?"

"Except, maybe we was in too big a hurry to run. I'm sure I saw some scalps sneak off into the brush. And what if Perkins is still alive?"

"He ain't," Yost said. "And I didn't see anyone else. Just the one I shot in the head. I guess we can go back, and if them riders didn't find him, we'll get his hair tomorrow."

"Hopefully, they left the wagons and horses," another of the men said.

"What do you figure, girly?" Yost asked as he jerked the dress from Bella's face.

Her chest crashed into itself, squeezing her heart and lungs as she cowered back.

He grinned and leaned in close until the stink of his foul body and his evil breath filled her head and blocked everything else. "We leave anyone else back there?"

She opened her eyes and shook her head.

He smiled and slapped her already battered face with his open palm, slamming her head against the ground.

Stars flashed across her eyes.

"We go back tomorrow and find you've lied, we won't be nice to you, like we been today."

The other men guffawed.

Yost cleared his throat and spat on her cheek. As the warm goo slithered down her face toward her neck, he tugged off his knee-length boots and reached for the buttons of his trousers. "I told you to get her legs."

"What's that?" one of the other men said.

Bella raised her head and glimpsed light flashing off distant leaves.

"Douse that fire," Yost said.

"Don't see it anymore. What was it?" one of the men asked.

"I said douse that fire. Now!" Yost said.

Two of the men kicked and scattered the coals from the fire ring and stomped on them as the third poured water from his canteen.

Yost tugged his boots back on, then stopped his foot mid-stomp. "Wait. Benny. Ev. Get the horses saddled. Cort, gag her and get her ready to ride." He scooped up a handful of dry twigs and tossed it onto the remains of the fire. As the dry tinder flared and the flames lit the surrounding trees, he picked up his rifle and moved to the edge of the little clearing. "We won't go far. Just ease off into the brush and wait for them to come to us."

"What if they ain't trailing us," Cort asked.

"Do what I told ya," Yost said. "There's no other reason for anyone to be out here." He hesitated, then chuckled. "If they ain't after us, I hope they've got black hair."

Bella scooched back as Cort reached for her.

He grinned, stood, and kicked her in the ribs, driving the air from her body. "Don't be like that, girly."

She curled into a ball and tried to take in a breath, but her lungs locked and panic coursed through her.

He grabbed her hair, jerked back her head, and forced his sour, sweat-stained bandana between her teeth.

Once her locked lungs relaxed, she sucked in air. Her nose, already full of dried blood, the air rushed in through the bandana. She gagged, choked, and hacked as the foul air entered her throat through the filthy scrap of cloth.

"Stop that or you'll get another kick," Cort said.

She fought her coughing into submission as he untied her hands from the tree and jerked her to her feet.

Yost threw an armful of dry branches onto the fire, then turned and led them through the trees and into the darkness. "Get her up on Perkins's horse," he said. "And tie her hands to the horn." He pulled a rope from one of the other saddles, looped it around her neck, and tied it to the trunk of a small tree. "You'd better keep quiet or that horse will move," he said. "He takes off, you'll lose your head."

Her heart thumped in her chest as she cast her eyes around. All four of her captors had taken their rifles and moved off into the underbrush. Yost was right. Whoever was coming had to be following them.... Coming to her rescue? But who? And how? It didn't matter. They were coming, and they were riding into a trap.

She had to warn them. But how? She looked down at the horse. It had already dropped its head and begun to graze. It took an easy step forward, drawing a few inches of slack out of the rope around her neck. She tried to say whoa, but it came out, "hoooo."

She bit down on the bandana with the strong, large teeth at the side of her mouth. She gagged and swallowed a cough as her mouth filled with saliva. She ground her molars back and forth. The well-worn, sun-bleached cotton of the bandana quickly gave way to her assault.

Once it felt like it was about to give, she whispered, "Whoa. Whoa." She leaned and strained and bent forward until she caught the bandana with her thumb at the corner of her mouth. "Hoooo."

She pulled back, and the bandana ripped, pulled out of her mouth, and hung from her thumb. She pressed all the air from her body, leaned down as far as she could, and touched the knot in the rope with her tongue. She felt her way along the loose end, then grasped the knot between her canine teeth. She wriggled and tugged until the rope slid.

Her heart soared. "Please, Saint Jude," she whispered to the heavens.

The horse stepped forward, searching for fresh grass, and the rope tightened around her neck enough to pull her teeth from the knot. No. Not now. "Whoa. Back," she whispered. The horse pulled up a mouthful of grass and chewed it, crunch, crunch, crunch.

She strained against the rope, letting the coarse fibers cut into the tender skin of her throat, but try as she might, she could no longer reach the rope with her teeth.

For a moment, all hope left her, and tears streamed down her cheeks. She thought of the girls, all alone at the side of the road, and she forced herself forward until the coarse rope dug deep into her throat, cutting off all air. Her head spun, but still she could not catch the knot with her teeth.

She sat back. She had to do something. Whoever it was coming through the trees was riding straight into a trap. She had to warn them. If she shouted, the horse might bolt, and even if he didn't, the men would come and silence her.

She listened to the sounds of the night. Yost and his men rustled around in a semicircle out away from her. The birds and insects of the night had gone silent at their intrusion.

She licked her lips and whistled. 'Whip-poor-will, whip-poor-will, whip-poor-will.' She paused and listened. The men had stopped rustling around, but no one approached her.

One of the men whispered. She couldn't make out the words, but at least some of the others moved south toward the whisperer.

Behind her, the fire cracked and popped. The horse took another easy step. Pulling her back against the cantle of the saddle. "Whoa. Easy."

Her thoughts raced. What could she do? She looked past her cheeks and pressed forward with her hands, hoping to create some slack around the saddle horn where the rope might slip off.

'Whip-poor-wiiiiiill,' she trilled. Hoping the approaching riders might, somehow, some way, hear the urgency in her bird call. 'Whip-poor-wiiiiiiiiiill.'

The horse took another step and stretched her neck and her arms to the limit.

CHAPTER nine

The sorrel stumbled, kept his feet, and galloped on. Carson took a deep breath and slowed down. He would do Bella no good if he crippled his big horse.

They stayed at the edge of the trees, and mostly in shadow, as they circled the clearing. The light of the fire flickered against the canopy of leaves above it, marking their destination.

Gate rode close and touched Carson's shoulder. "They'll be waiting for us," he whispered. "We'll leave the horses and go on foot."

Carson nodded.

As they snuck through the trees and brush toward the fire, Carson marveled at how Gate moved without a single brush of a branch against his buckskin clothes or pop of a twig under his moccasined feet. Carson held his rifle in one hand and eased apart the brush with his other. He felt, as best he could, through his boot soles before putting down his weight. And still, he could not move like the older man.

A whip-poor-will sang out. Gate froze. When it sang again, he motioned for Carson to move away to the west, then he moved off to the northeast.

The whip-poor-will sang again. Gate froze, shook his head, caught Carson's eye, and gently cocked his Winchester.

Carson cocked his own rifle.

Gate moved forward, then froze and held his left hand to his ear.

Carson did the same.

As Carson paused, Gate moved forward and listened again. When Gate stopped, Carson moved.

They continued for several cycles of listening and moving until a horse snorted. Carson's heart jumped, and he dropped into a crouch.

Gate melted deep into the shadows of a large hickory.

Careful not to make a sound, Carson eased in behind the nearest oak, leaned in against it, then peeked around. The horse blew again. A man whispered. Someone moved through the trees toward him. He took his rifle in both hands and pressed himself against the rough bark.

A short, spare man stepped from the shadows and into a pocket of moonlight.

Carson raised his rifle and took a half step from the tree. "U.S. Marshals. Drop that rifle!"

The man dove for cover, firing a shot as he went.

Carson fired two quick shots into the clump of brush where the man had disappeared.

The man grunted on the second shot as Carson ducked back in behind the oak.

Behind him, the night erupted into crashes of rifle fire and flashing streaks of flame from rifle barrels.

Carson spotted a bright muzzle blast, aimed beyond it, and fired. His bullet thwapped into flesh, and the firing stopped.

The sound of a single horse crashing away through the brush filled the night.

Carson stepped around the tree.

"Stay covered," Gate shouted.

Carson ducked back.

"Could be someone playin' possum. How many you hit?"

"Two. At least I think so."

"I got one for sure."

"Leaves one. And Bella."

Gate ducked low and sprinted over to Carson. "When I start shooting, stay low and get to that next tree." He leaned out and fired, levered his rifle, and fired again.

Carson hustled forward and in against the next big tree. No one shot back.

"Now you shoot," Gate said.

Carson fired his rifle, once, twice, and again.

Gate pressed in against him. "They're down or gone."

Horses pounded off to the west.

Carson started forward, then turned back toward the horses, then stopped. "Let's make sure the three we shot are dead, then go for the horses."

Gate grabbed his sleeve. "You bring both horses. I'll check the bodies."

CHAPTER ten

After Bella's last, begging, whip-poor-will cry, the horse raised his head and extended his neck forward. Already stretched back to the end of her arms, the rope around her neck began to cut off her breath, and her vision whirled and spun. She lifted her heels to the animal's shoulders. With her father, she had once watched a famous horseman put on a display of bridleless riding. The man had pressed his heels into his mount's shoulders and backed him all the way across the pen. She was no horse trainer, but if the horse took another step forward, she would surely die.

The horse looked around, then lowered his head and reached for the next clump of grass. As he leaned forward, Bella's neck and back stretched further than ever before. She croaked air through her constricted throat. "Whoa." And bumped her heels against the horse's shoulders. "Back."

The horse's head popped up.

Blackness swept into the edges of Bella's swirling vision. "Back," she said, one final time, as her consciousness slipped further and further away.

The last thing she heard as she slid into blackness was the crashing of branches, and a faint, distant voice hissing "Get back."

When she came back to herself, her entire body ached. Something or someone pounded her middle. Hooves pounding the ground below her told her she lay, face-down, on a running horse. Had they saved her? She forced her eyes open. The thick greasy trouser leg and the knee-high boot told her all she needed to know.

She felt a big hand against her back as the saddle horn pounded her middle. She wiggled her toes. If she threw herself back and off the horse, could she run? Would her legs even work? Were the other's, whoever they might be, following behind?

As the horse ducked and weaved through the trees, she tried to see past Yost's leg. The horse's ribs pumped in and out like rasping bellows and his breath came in great gasps. Yost was running scared. Someone was coming. Hope filled her.

She tensed her muscles to throw herself back and off the horse, but before she gathered the strength, Yost clutched the back of her dress and threw her to the ground. Rifle in hand, he stepped off the slowing horse and stumbled to a stop as the horse galloped on. He spun around, grabbed her by the hair, and dragged her in behind a huge, old oak tree.

She pushed herself to her knees, then struggled to her feet and took a staggering, pain-filled step.

The rope around her neck jerked tight, slamming her to the ground on her back.

"You stay there, and not a sound," Yost said, "Or I swear, I'll cut your throat right now." Leading with his rifle, he leaned out around the rough tree trunk.

Bella rolled onto her belly, wriggled forward, and peeked back the way they had just come.

Yost stepped on her back and pressed her into the acorns and leaves under the oak. "Stay, right there, girlie, and not a squeak. I hear them coming."

Carson and Gate galloped over a small rise.

Yost breathed out and squeezed the trigger.

As the hammer fell, Bella pushed up with all the strength she had left.

Yost stumbled out from behind the tree, and his shot flew high. He levered his Winchester and ducked back, as shots from Carson and Gate slammed into the tree trunk.

"That you, Yost?" Gate shouted.

Pain blinded Bella when the rope around her neck tightened against her torn skin as Yost hoisted her to her feet. "I got me a pretty little girly here. You let me go and I'll set her free down the trail."

Gate laughed. "I've known you too long to believe that. You might leave me a scalped corpse, but I wouldn't expect any more."

"I give you my word," Yost said. "I'll leave her a mile along the trail. Long as I don't see or hear you coming. After that you can chase me all you want."

Gate chuckled, but there was no humor in his voice. "Let me talk it over with the deputy here."

"You'd best talk fast. I'm feeling bloody."

*****

His Sharps cradled in his elbows, Carson crawled on his belly through the dry creek bed until he was well into the trees beyond the path they had followed and out of sight of Bella and her captor, the man Gate had called Yost. He snaked forward until he could peer through the leaves and make out the outline of a big man with his arm clasped around Bella's neck.

Gate leaned out from the tree where he hid and shouted, "How do we know you'll let her go?"

As Yost leaned to the far side of the oak to reply, Carson darted across a patch of open ground, dropped in behind a fallen log. Resting the back of his hand on the rough bark, he laid the forestock of the Sharps onto his palm.

Through the telescope mounted on his rifle, he saw the big, rust-bearded man with his left arm around Bella's neck, squeezing her close. Moving down, the polished glass magnified every scrap, bruise, and swollen spot on Bella's face and neck.

Rage coursed from deep within Carson's body; as it came to the surface, his body shook all over. He couldn't risk a shot, not shaking this way. Not with Bella so close. He took one deep breath and then another. He focused on the movement and the slight snick as he eased back the hammer, then he placed all his attention on the tiny click as he pulled the rear set trigger.

The big man shouted. "I'll cut her throat, Gate. You know I will."

Carson's focus narrowed until every thought, every feeling, every sound melted into his right eye. His body stopped shaking, and his world became deathly still. He released the air from his lungs in one smooth, slow motion. Near the end of his exhalation, he squeezed.

*****

Bella prayed to herself. "Please, God, don't let him take me. Please don't let him take me. Surely Carson and Gate found the children. Surely, they're safe. Please let them be safe. Don't let him take me. Let him kill me right here."

Yost's head jerked back and forth, and a loud bang shattered the early morning air. His meaty arm slid from her neck, and he slumped to the ground.

Stunned, Bella glanced toward the sound of the rifle shot.

Carson peeked over his rifle. "Is he dead?"

She dropped her eyes and ran them from the high boots, up the filthy trousers, past the blood-and-grease-stained shirt to Yost's head. The one eye, she could see, stared toward the tree. A bloodless hole, maybe the width of her thumb, pierced the skin and bone at Yost's temple. Blood and brain matter splattered the ground around his greasy hair.

She stumbled away from the grisly scene. "He's dead," she said, as she stood tottering, unsure if she could stay on her feet.

Carson leaped over the log and sprinted toward her. "Bella!"

She took a step toward him, every ounce of her wanting his comfort. Then she stiffened and turned her face away.

He threw his arms around her.

Sobs wracked her body. She pushed him away. "Leave me be."

He stiffened, but held on.

"They.... They.... I tried to stop them, but they...." The rest of the words hung in her throat and twisted like a spear through her heart.

Carson placed his hand against the back of her head and gently pulled her face toward his shoulder.

She stiffened and pushed back against his hand.

Gentle but firm, he held her close. "You didn't do anything wrong. All four of them are dead."

She softened her neck, dropped her face into the junction of his shoulder and his neck, wrapped her arms around his muscular body, and sobbed.

His touch feather-like, he stroked her hair, over and over and over. "It'll be all right. It's going to be all right. You're safe."

Most of her doubted his gentle whispers and soothing caresses, but deep inside, a tiny spark of hope burned through the darkness.

CHAPTER eleven

Patricia and Britt peered through the leaves of a low-lying shrub on a small hill. A hundred yards below, six mud and stick shanties spread across a small clearing. Around the shanties, women and children and old men went about their daily business. To the right, three women talked and smiled as they scraped meat and fat from a staked-out deer hide. Four little boys poked sticks at a tied-up dog and laughed when it snapped at them. An old man sat cross-legged against one of the shanties, watching the boys torment the dog. Beside him, a young woman suckled a baby.

Patricia and Britt pushed back from the brow of the hill. And once they were far enough to be out of sight of the Wichita people in the village, they both stood and trotted down the hill to where Remy and Horace waited with the horses.

Patricia spoke first. "We'll shoot as many as we can from up above, then ride down and finish the rest." She turned toward Britt. "Take Remy around to the other side."

Britt grinned and nodded.

"We'll wait for you to shoot. Remember, no one escapes."

Britt motioned toward the horses with his head. "Come on, Remy."

Though it had been only minutes, time dragged as Patricia fingered the forestock of her Winchester. What was keeping them? She took a deep breath, settled onto her belly, laid the front sight of her rifle on the woman nursing the baby, then moved it to the old man and back. If she was quick enough, she could get them both before they realized what was happening.

She shook her head and settled on a woman who sat shucking corn near a small garden patch closer to the edge of the village. She would leave the old man to lead the others across the clearing.

After that, it would be a matter of finding a target and taking it out.

She smiled and remembered when she was thirteen. Uncle Cliff had backed a wagon down a rocky hill and poured a barrel of water into the den of an old she-wolf. The wolf had taken cattle for years and they had finally found her den.

Her father whispered, "There should be the bitch and five pups. I'll leave them all to you, unless they spread out too much, but I expect they'll run right along that hillside. Take the she-wolf last. Let her lead them along, or they'll scatter."

Her hands had trembled a little as Uncle Cliff had poured the water, but today, they were rock steady.

The she-wolf had burst out first, chased by her four half-grown pups. Patricia missed the first shot in her haste. She levered in another round and hit the lead pup. The three pups behind it leaped over the tumbling body. By the time she'd shot the rest of the pups, the old wolf was close to two hundred yards away. She swung her rifle out ahead of the fast-moving, low-slung creature. Her bullet kicked up dust three feet behind the wolf's tail.

Her father's bullet hit the wolf in the shoulders and tumbled her head over tail to the ground.

Anger coursed through Patricia. Why had he shot? She would have corrected her aim and hit the wolf with her next shot. Then shame filled her, she'd let her father down. It was one thing to miss a sprinting, ducking, diving jackrabbit, but a straight-running, three-and-a-half-foot-tall wolf?

Her father jumped to his feet, his face beaming with joy. "Wow! Did you see that, Cliff? Patty got 'em all but the bitch."

Uncle Cliff threw his hat in the air. "That was some shooting."

She fought down her joy and pushed to her feet, pulled a round from her pocket, and slid it into the rifle.

Her father took the rifle and let it drop onto the grassy hill. For one of the few times in her life, he threw his arms around her shoulders and twirled her feet off the ground. "Couldn't have done better myself," he said.

Britt's shot jerked her from the memory.

Before the woman shucking the corn could react, Patricia's rifle barked, and the woman threw up her hands, throwing the cob of corn into the air.

Sure enough, the old man jumped to his feet, shouted, and waved, leading the others toward the woods beyond the garden.

Patricia swung her rifle past him and shot the woman with the baby, then onto the boy with the stick. Several other old men and women scrambled out of the shanties. One man, with long gray braids, stepped around his hut and pointed his rifle up the hill toward Britt and Remy. Patricia's bullet struck him in the middle of the back. She swung the rifle toward an old woman, hobbling along toward the trees, but before she could pull the trigger, Horace's rifle barked, and the old woman tumbled to the ground.

She swung toward the old man, but he'd been quicker than she expected, and before she could find him with her front sight, he and two young boys disappeared into the trees. "Get around them," she shouted. "No one escapes." She turned to Horace. "Get the horses." As he ran down the hill, she started after the old man and the boys.

Horace slid his horse to a stop beside her and handed her the reins to her own horse.

She shouted, "Take a big circle, then light the brush. Wind's right. We'll smoke them out. Tell Britt. I'll wait here."

Horace nodded and galloped away.

She ground tied her horse, sprinted to the top of the highest hill, sat, and waited. Minutes later, smoke and ash, carried on the gusty west wind, burned her eyes and nose. She wiped away tears and kept her eyes on the treeline.

Someone shouted, and she swung her rifle toward the shout and a flash of movement. One boy darted into the open. Her first shot hit him low and dropped him. He clawed at the ground, trying to pull himself back into the trees. Her second shot pinned him to the ground for good.

The old man appeared, then ducked back before she could shoot. He flashed into the open a few strides north, then again ducked back.

Flame showed in the treetops over the dense smoke. Before long, the old man and the remaining boy would have to show themselves or die in the inferno.

Once again, the old man appeared. This time she got off a shot, but her bullet flew wide, and he was back in the trees before she could shoot again. While she watched for the old man, a flash of blue caught her eye as the boy sprinted from one patch of trees to the next.

The old man shouted, pulling her eyes from the sprinting boy. She shot the old man and turned back. The boy was gone.

Thick smoke from flames in the tall grass at the bottom of the hill enveloped her and forced her to forget about the boy and run for her life.

Her horse had broken his ground tie and trotted away from the smoke. "Whoa," she shouted.

The horse hesitated, then continued trotting. He stepped on a rein and jerked the bit in his mouth.

"Whoa!"

This time, he stopped.

She scooped up the reins, swung into the saddle, and galloped in the direction the boy had run.

They searched for the boy for half an hour until Patricia fired a shot into the air. "Come on in, boys."

Once the men had gathered around her, she said, "We'll have to let him go. We'd better get out of here before the young bucks from the village or someone else sees this smoke and comes to check it out." She led them across the blackened hillside, winding around the spots still smoldering and smoking. The fire had split and left the tiny village intact. "Make sure there's no one in those huts and take the scalps. We need to hurry."

A baby crying led her to the body of the child's mother. Patricia stepped to the ground and knelt beside the wailing infant.

Beside her, Britt peeled the ears and the hair from the baby's mother. "Kill it. We need to get out of here."

Patricia looked at the baby, then back at Britt. "Go on. I'll be right there. Head toward Burnett's. We'll stick to the plan. "

By the time she caught up with her men. The rocking of the loping horse had calmed and quieted the baby, swaddled and tucked into the crook of her left arm.

Britt looked over as she rode up beside him. "No! What are you doing?"

What was she doing? She knew she couldn't keep the little she-creature, but.... She looked at Britt. "I couldn't do it."

Britt pushed his horse against hers. "Give it to me."

She shook her head, pressed a heel into her horse's side, and pushed it away.

"Patty," Britt said. "This ain't smart. Give me that pup."

Her eyes turned hard. "I'm still the boss here. I'll worry about this baby. You boys take care of things at Burnett's like we planned."

Britt shook his head and started his horse away. "Your pa won't like this."

Minutes later, they rode down the steep hill leading to the Red River. Patricia hesitated, then twisted the baby up and around, until the little, black-haired head rested against her shoulder. She rode into the river.

By the time they splashed out onto the Texas side, the baby howled its discomfort.

"Give me that thing," Brit said.

Patricia turned her hard eyes on him. "Go on and take care of things at Burnett's like I told you."

Britt muttered under his breath. "Won't always be like this." He turned to the other men. "Come on."

Patricia knew next to nothing about babies, but she stepped from her horse, laid the child in the crook of her arm, and swung it back and forth. "Don't cry. Please don't cry. What do you want?"

Her nose told her one thing the baby needed. She unwrapped the soft rabbit fur swaddling the baby and pulled away the swatch of cotton from the infant's bottom. "Hey there. Don't cry. I'll clean you up, little girl."

Using the soiled rag and handfuls of grass, she cleaned the little dimpled bottom and wrapped it in dry grass and her own bandana. But the baby still cried. "You must be hungry, but you'll have to wait." She stuck her pinky into the little mouth, and the baby sucked and slurped. A primal warmth flooded her body.

By the time she rode over the hill above the Burnett's little homestead, the boys had done their work. Tall, muscular, young David Burnett's body sprawled in the yard, his head scalped, but Indian style, taking the hair but leaving the ears.

Beyond him, Mary Burnett lay naked, abused, and also scalped, just like they'd planned.

Patricia swallowed back the bile in her throat and looked down at the baby sleeping in the crook of her left arm. "It's dirty business, but it had to be done. Can't have nesters fencing the range to keep our cows off of their crops." She fingered the infant's fine hair. "Nesters are like nits. Start out with one or two, and if you don't comb them out right away, next thing you know, your head's crawling with them. Besides, today, we killed two birds with one stone."

When the boys looked up at her, she waved her arm toward the west and started down the hill. Instead of going east back to the ranch, they would ride out into the rocky breaks and lose their tracks before returning home.

She caught up to the men as they hustled their horses toward the southwest. She turned to Britt. "Did you leave those Wichita scalps?"

He looked at her like she was addled. "Wasn't that the plan?"

She nodded. "Just checking. Didn't hide them too deep, I hope."

"I hung the fresh ones on nails in the barn, like they was there to dry, and put the salted ones in a pile on the workbench."

"Smart," she said. For a moment, she glanced at Britt's square jaw and strong, wide shoulders. The major flashed into her mind. A war hero. A man of books. A man who loved a woman so much that he still grieved and visited her grave every day. Britt was nothing compared to a man like that. Britt was a tool and nothing more. She needed to make her father see that

CHAPTER twelve

Though she had stayed in her room and had not seen them since arriving at the fort, the mere thought of Phillip's four daughters kept Bella from toppling headlong and forever into despair. She stood back and stared out the window at them, running and laughing. It amazed her how resilient they were, after first losing their mother, and then what they saw back on the road.

Major Kinsey knocked on the door to his own office, pushed it open and backed through, carrying a tray holding a teapot and two mugs. He glanced at her and smiled. "I thought we might have a cup of tea while we talk."

For maybe the first time since it all happened three days prior, she felt a slight lifting of the corners of her mouth and eyes.

He nodded toward a chair on the far side of the little table, then set down the tray and poured the smoky brew into the fine porcelain cups.

"Honey?" he asked, then before she could answer, his cheeks reddened. "I like mine with honey."

She nodded.

"Cream?"

She nodded again, and her mouth watered as he spooned a dollop of thick, rich cream into her cup, gave it a quick stir, and slid it toward her.

She waited for him to prepare his own cup and sit, then she lifted the cup to her mouth. She paused and breathed in the earthy, smoky fragrance, then blew across the steaming surface and took a small sip.

She longed to tell him it was delicious—to thank him for his kindness and for the care and attention he lavished on Phillip's girls, but her tongue failed her, and she planted her eyes on the table and took another sip.

"What do you think?" he asked. "Do you like it?"

She nodded. "Yes, thank you."

"I'm glad you agreed to see me," he said. "I want you to know that, despite how it feels, you're not alone."

She nodded and said, "Thank you." Though the hole left by her father's murder felt as if it was too wide and too deep to ever cross.

"I know it's only been three days, but have you had time to think about your future."

In an instant, the blood rushed to her face, and she clenched her fists. Of course she'd thought about it. Other than the children, she'd thought of nothing else. She wanted to lash out at him, somehow make this kind man pay for all that she'd lost.

Just as quickly, the anger drained down her body and out through the floor. She dropped her face into her hands and choked back a sob.

His chair scraped across the floor, and she felt him move to stand beside her.

For a moment he stood silent and unmoving. His hand touched her shoulder. "I understand loss," he said. "You're welcome to stay here for as long as you need, but, well, this is no place for a young woman."

"I don't know what to do.... I don't know if I can even go on."

He squeezed her shoulder. "People care about you. The girls ask about you every day. They miss you."

Her belly tightened, and she scrubbed her hands over her face. Of course, they would miss her. They needed her, but what could she tell them? And what if, oh please God, don't let it be, but what if she was with child, and not even a true child, not a child of love, but the spawn of one of those devils.

She burst into loud sobs.

The major dropped to his knees beside her and pulled her against his side. "I know it doesn't seem like it, but..."

The door to his office burst open.

"Oh my," a woman said. "I'm sorry to interrupt, but there was no one at the desk and I.... I brought your book and I need...."

A baby began to wail, and Bella glanced through her hair at a tall, fine-featured young woman about her own age holding a swaddled baby in the crook of one arm and two books in the other hand.

The major jumped to his feet. "Miss Grimwald."

The young woman glanced toward the door.

"Come in. Join us. Well, I suppose I should ask," he said, turning to Bella. "Do you mind if Miss Grimwald joins us? She's a friend and lives across the river in Texas."

Bella was about to stand and excuse herself when the baby stopped wailing and found her eyes with its own dark orbs. Something inside her melted as she locked onto the little round face. She nodded and said, "Please join us."

"Sit," the major said. "I'll find another cup."

"I don't want to interrupt," Patricia said. "I'll come back."

"Please stay," Bella said. Wiping her eyes on her sleeve. "Don't mind me."

"Are you sure?" Patricia asked. "I can leave the books and come back later."

Bella forced a weak smile. "Your baby's got good lungs."

Patricia looked down at the baby in her arms. "It's not.... Well, I suppose.... Anyway, that's what I came to talk to you about, Major."

"Let me find that cup, the major said. "Sit. Let me introduce you. Patricia Grimwald, this is Bella Foresti. Miss Foresti, Miss Grimwald."

Patricia laughed. "So formal, Major. Y'all can both call me Patricia."

The major turned and hurried out of the room.

Patricia sat in his chair across from Bella.

"What's your baby's name?" Bella asked.

"Oh my," Patricia said, "She's not mine. She's a little Wichita I found out on the prairie."

Bella raised one eyebrow. "How did she get there?"

Patricia shook her head. "I don't suppose you heard about what's been going on around here." She touched her mouth with her right hand. "Oh my. Excuse me. Of course, you have." She glanced at the ceiling. "I suspect she came from a Wichita village, down along the river west of here. I call her Perdita."

"You couldn't find her people?"

Patricia glanced at the ceiling, then lowered her eyes. "It appears the nesters killed them."

The major returned, set a third cup, saucer, and spoon onto the table and pulled up a chair.

As he poured, Patricia asked Bella, "How do you like the Lapsang Souchong?"

Bella hesitated.

"The tea," Patricia said. "The major's father gets it from a Dutch trader in Boston and has it shipped to him all the way out here." She smiled at the major and touched his forearm. "I, for one, love it."

The baby mewled, and her face darkened.

Patricia frowned. "Here she goes again. I'm afraid she's hungry, but I've no experience with such things." She turned to the major. "I was hoping you might convince the trader to find me a nurse maid amongst the Indians. I'd ask him myself, but you know how he feels about my father, and well, I suppose all of us." She smiled a brief smile. "Me too."

The baby sucked in a deep breath and began to wail.

Bella stood and reached her arms across the table. "May I?"

Patricia thrust the squalling baby toward Bella. "Be my guest."

Bella pulled the baby against her shoulder and breast, cupped the back of the tiny head with one hand, and bounced around the room, cooing and whispering to the infant. As she breathed in the clean scent of the little head, her chest and shoulders softened just a touch.

Patricia leaned close to the major. Bella picked up a word here and there. Something about nesters, and killings, and impending war.

The baby relaxed and fell quiet.

"I'm sure you agree the land around here's too rich, too fertile, to be left to a bunch of heathens," Patricia said. "My father asked me to implore you, to beg if I have to, to convince the powers that be to move the savages further north and west, before the entire country descends into war."

Not wanting to hear about any more death or destruction, Bella focused on the baby. She dipped her pinky into the little flowered pitcher of cream and placed it against the infant's lips.

The tiny pink tongue probed the cream. Then the soft lips parted, and the baby slurped in Bella's fingertip.

Bella pulled out her finger with a slight pop. The baby wrinkled her brow until Bella dipped her finger back into the cream and returned it to the tiny girl's lips.

Major Kinsey chuckled. "You've got a way with her."

Hot blood rushed to Bella's cheeks. She glanced at the cream pitcher. "I'm so sorry. I..."

Major Kinsey's smile lit his face. "Never mind that. There's lots more cream where that came from. You know babies."

Patricia nodded to Bella and turned to the major. "She does, doesn't she?" She touched the back of Major Kinsey's arm and pressed him toward the door, then met Bella's eyes. "Would you mind watching her for a few minutes, while the major and I discuss business?"

Bella glanced down at the little black-haired head. "Not at all."

"Are you sure?" Major Kinsey asked.

Bella nodded.

"We'll talk more later," he said.

Once they had left the room, Bella continued to feed cream from the pitcher until the tiny girl turned away and yawned.

Ten minutes later, someone knocked on the door. "Major Kinsey?" Carson asked through the door.

The doorknob turned

Heart racing, Bella looked around the room. There was nowhere to hide. She started to speak, but the words caught in her throat. As the door opened a crack, she cleared her throat and said, "He's not here."

Carson opened the door and stepped part way in. "Bella?"

"He's not here."

Carson stepped fully into the room. "I've been trying to see you."

"I'll bet they've gone to the dining hall."

Carson stepped forward, leaving the door open. "Who have you got there?"

Bella glanced at the baby sleeping in her arms. She fought to hold back a sob, afraid it would wake the sleeping girl. Tears flooded from the corners of her eyes. She turned toward the big bookshelf. "Just leave me be, Deputy."

His footsteps sounded on the plank floor. Had he gone?

Her breath caught and her heart leaped as he reached past her arm and stroked the baby's downy head.

His warm breath stirred the stray hairs touching her cheek. "What's her name?"

Why couldn't he just leave her alone..., get on with his marshal business, and leave her with her sorrow?

"She's soft."

"Her name's Perdita. She's all alone. Just like me."

Carson pulled his hand from the baby's head and laid it against Bella's cheek. "I'm so sorry for what happened. We should have stayed with you. I didn't know...."

Her heart raced and felt like it might burst from her chest. Was it anger or something else? She glanced up at his fine face. "Wasn't your fault. Wasn't anyone's fault, but those that did it, and those that paid them for scalps."

He slid his arm around her and eased her shoulder against his chest. "The children are worried about you."

She glanced toward the window.

"Phillip's worried about you." He cleared his throat. "I've been worried about you too."

She met his eyes, then let her head relax onto his strong shoulder.

He reached around the back of her head and cradled her there against him.

The dam inside her burst, and tears poured out onto his shirt. She tried to lean away, but he gently held her close, and for a few moments, wrapped her in his warm caring.

The unlatched door burst open and Major Kinsey and Patricia burst into the room. The major slid to a stop. "I'm sorry. I didn't..."

Bella jerked away from Carson, turned toward the bookshelf, and scrubbed the tears from her cheeks with one sleeve of her dress.

"I didn't know you were back," Major Kinsey said.

Carson cleared his throat. "Just got here and came to report."

Patricia stepped past Major Kinsey. "Did you find out if any of the other farmers were involved in the scalping and killing?"

Carson looked from the major to Patricia. "Well. Um.... We..."

Major Kinsey met Bella's eyes and said, "Let's not discuss this now."

Patricia nodded. "Oh yes. You're right. I'm sorry Bella." She stepped toward Carson and held out her hand like a man. "I'm Patricia Grimwald."

Carson shook the outstretched hand. "Carson Kettle."

"The famous deputy that brought Lijah Penne to Justice."

Carson's cheeks turned pink. "Not so famous."

"Did you find any survivors at the Wichita village?"

Carson glanced at the major. "One small boy."

All the color left Patricia's cheeks. "Did he say what happened?"

"He may be a mute, or maybe he's just frightened, but he hasn't said a word."

CHAPTER thirteen

Patricia paced around the small room, Major Kinsey always made available for her when she visited Fort Sill. Her boots clicked on the spotless plank floor. She reached over the vase of wildflowers on the table in front of the window, pushed aside the heavy canvas curtains, and peered out at the soldiers marching on the hard-packed red clay of the parade ground. Even with the door and window closed, the barking commands of the drill sergeant grated against her mind, but she paid no attention to the words. She dropped the curtain, marched the two strides back across the room, and flopped onto the metal army cot and the rough, wool blanket.

The door burst open, and Britt burst in. He frowned as she sat up.

"What?" she asked.

"We ain't got time for a nap."

"I'm not napping. I'm thinking."

"What's to think about? We kill the boy and that's that."

"Did you find him?"

He shook his head. "Haven't seen him, but I hear that Quaker Indian agent has him."

"Can we get to him?"

Britt shook his head. "We'd need some kind of distraction."

"What's the worst he could say?"

"He could probably identify us all if he saw us."

She tugged at her chin. "White folk are probably all the same to him."

"And if he points us out?"

"Like I always say, act surprised, look concerned, deny, deny, deny."

Britt stepped closer. "I say tonight we have the boys light something back of the Quaker's house on fire, then slip in and knock the little rat on the head."

She paused. "We need to carry him off first. Make it look like he ran away."

Britt turned toward the window, pulled a yellow flower from the vase on the table, and held it to his nose. "Ain't this nice?"

"You know I don't care about things like that."

"The major leave 'em for you?"

Her cheeks warmed. "What if he did?"

"Don't be getting any foolish ideas." He crossed the room, sat on the bed beside her, grabbed the back of her head, and pulled her lips to his.

She shoved him away. "What are you doing?"

"Claiming what's mine."

She thrust him away and jumped up off the bed.

He laughed. "Don't be like that. Your daddy and me got big plans for you, and they don't include no fancy eastern soldier boy."

She sucked in a deep breath. "Neither you nor my father have any business making plans for me."

He grinned and patted the blanket beside him. "Awe, come on. Don't be like that. You used to like a little slap and tickle."

"Used to is the key," she said.

Britt's smile fled, and his face darkened. He held her eyes with his own narrow gaze.

Unblinking, she matched his stare.

Someone pounded on the door.

Patricia tore her eyes from Britt's. "Who is it?"

"Remy. Y'all better come."

Patricia looked at Britt. "What's going on?" By the time she turned back to Remy, he had disappeared. And by the time she and Britt hit the door, Remy was halfway down the hill to the edge of the fort.

They rounded the corner to the Indian agent's trading post. Two soldiers held Horace by the arms, and the short, rotund agent stood before him, waving a finger just off Horace's nose.

Horace stood, wide-eyed and red-faced.

"What are you doing? Let him go," Patricia shouted.

Horace turned his head and saw her. "I didn't..."

"Quiet, Horace," Patricia shouted. She turned toward the agent. "What's the meaning of this? Let him go. Someone get the major."

The short agent puffed up. "Already sent for."

Major Kinsey trotted around the corner, followed by two privates. He glanced at Patricia, then at the agent. "What is it, Josiah?"

The red-faced agent waddled up to the major. "It's the boy.... Well, you see, the boy was watching out the window, and well...," he pointed at Horace. "This one walked by and the boy ducked back and when Martha asked what was wrong, he pointed out the window at this one."

Horace turned to Patricia. "I didn't..."

"I told you to be quiet," she said. She turned to the major. "Surely, a boy pointing out the window is no reason for these men to rough up my hand."

The major turned to the soldiers holding Horace. "She's right. Let him go." He turned to the agent. "Bring out the boy, and Martha."

Patricia's thoughts raced. What if the boy identified them all? "This is ridiculous. Horace hasn't been away from the rest of us for months. I bet the boy can't tell one white man in a red shirt from another." She turned to Horace. "Come on. We're leaving."

The major turned to her. "Please, Patricia. Let's clear this up right now."

She shook her head. "You'd take the word of a frightened little boy over my man's? Or mine?"

The major's cheeks reddened. "It's not that, but I don't want there to be a cloud over anyone."

Martha, the round-faced Wichita nursemaid, her straight, black hair framing her face, led a small black-headed boy from the trading post. As they exited the building, the boy glanced at the crowd that had gathered and turned back toward the store.

Martha held on, squatted, and pulled the boy around until he faced her. She took both his cheeks in her hands and tried to get him to look at her, but he kept his eyes locked on the ground.

Major Kinsey stepped forward. "Ask him if he knows this man," he said, pointing at Horace.

"This is foolishness. Come on, Horace. Britt. Remy. We're going home," Patricia said.

As Horace turned to follow her, the major nodded at the privates still flanking him.

They grabbed his arms.

"Ask him," the major said to Martha.

Martha leaned close to the boy and whispered into his ear.

At first the boy shook his head.

Martha again leaned in and whispered.

This time the boy glanced out the corner of his eye from Horace to Britt to Remy and finally to Patricia. When the boy's eyes flitted onto her, Patricia marched toward him. "This is craziness, Major. You're scaring the poor child." She crouched down and stroked the boy's head, now tucked tight into Martha's skirt. "Y'all know it was the nesters that killed this boy's people."

The boy trembled under her touch.

Patricia softened her eyes and glanced up at the major. "Think about it. Would I have saved that Wichita baby, left all alone on the prairie, if my men were slaughtering her people? It makes no sense."

Major Kinsey met her eyes. "You're right, but please. Let Martha ask him. For me."

Patricia's heart raced as she pulled her hands from the dark hair, stood, and stepped back two paces.

Martha squatted, stroked the boy's head, and spoke to him in Wichita.

The boy took a breath as if about to speak, then glanced up at Patricia, shook his head and ducked his face back into Martha's skirt. The pungent smell of urine filled the air as a puddle formed at the child's feet.

Patricia looked at Major Kinsey. "Look what you're doing to this poor child."

Major Kinsey hesitated, then looked from Patricia to the agent to Martha. "She's right, take him back inside."

The agent began to speak, but the major held an upturned hand to his face and nodded toward the door. "Martha. Take him back inside and clean him up." The major glanced at Patricia, then marched over to the agent, leaned in, and spoke.

Patricia held her breath and tried, but failed, to hear the words.

An hour later, Patricia stood just inside the door to the long wooden stable where the cavalrymen kept their mounts. Her carriage stood off to one side of the big barn doors.

Britt led his saddled horse behind the long row of swishing tails. Remy and Horace followed.

When Britt reached her, Patricia stuck her head out of the stable and glanced both ways. "Soon as you get home, send Uncle Cliff back."

Britt's eyes hardened. "You need to come with us now. The boy's as likely to identify you as any of us."

She shook her head. "I've got more to do here. I need to find out what those deputies are up to and I need to keep the major on our side."

Britt spit. "So that's it." He turned and looked at Horace and Remy. "Harness the carriage horses. Patricia's coming with us."

Waves of fire rushed up her body. "You'll do no such thing."

Britt grabbed her elbow and squeezed. "Harness them nags. Now!"

Patricia twisted away and barked at Horace and Remy. "Do as I say!"

Carson, coming from the major's office, walked around the corner. His eyes widened. "Everything all right?"

Patricia ran her hands down her dress, smoothing the rich fabric. She summoned a dazzling smile. "Why yes, Deputy. Everything's fine. The boys are just heading back to the ranch. We just got a herd of new cows and they need tending."

Carson looked at Britt, then back at Patricia. "I was hoping to have a word with you."

Britt glared. "She's got nothing to say to you."

"Britt!" Patricia said. "Why would you say that?" She brushed past Britt and took Carson's arm. "I'd be happy to speak with a handsome deputy like you. Lead on."

Carson led her toward the administration building.

Her mind raced. What did this strong young deputy want? Did he suspect her? First things first. She glanced over her shoulder and flicked her head south toward her father's ranch.

CHAPTER fourteen

Six cavalrymen mounted on fit, shiny horses trotted along the narrow road toward them. Carson eased Patricia to the side of the dusty road and nodded to the Sergeant leading the group.

With little more than a glance at the mounted men, Patricia continued to pepper him with questions. "And what about a young lady?" she asked with a smile.

When he stepped back toward the middle of the road, she flowed with him, her warm shoulder against his, and the clean fresh smell of her hair filling his nose.

"Deputy?" she asked.

"Sorry," Carson said. "I didn't hear you."

"I asked if you have a young lady waiting for you back in Fort Smith."

Carson shook his head and looked at the ground.

"Surely that can't be true. A handsome young hero, such as yourself."

"I'm no hero."

"Nonsense," she said, squeezing his arm even tighter. "Everyone knows what you did bringing Lijah Penne to the hangman."

"I had a lot of help with that."

They mounted the steps and entered the administration building. Carson nodded at the adjutant seated behind the desk in the foyer, then glanced at the major's office and wondered if Bella was still there. He led Patricia toward an open door on the other side of the foyer.

Marty met them at the door and stepped to one side to let Patricia enter.

"Another handsome deputy," she said. "It must be my lucky day."

Marty's freckled cheeks reddened as he pointed to the single wooden chair in front of the desk.

Once she sat, Carson took the chair directly behind the desk and Marty a seat off to the side.

She frowned. "So formal. I thought you might be inviting me for a cup of tea."

Carson took a deep breath. He hesitated. He wasn't used to giving orders. "Tea would be nice." He turned to Marty. "Would you mind?"

Once Marty had left the room, Carson cleared his throat and turned toward Patricia.

Before he could speak, she said, "What's this about, Deputy? Surely you can't think I, or any of my men, had anything to do with that Wichita village."

"Well, it's not that... It's just that... Well, the boy. He seems to think your man Horace was there."

She sat up straight. "Well, I can assure you he was with the rest of us. Did I tell you we just took delivery of a thousand head of cattle? I did, didn't I? Well, with all that, we had no time for anything but settling, those animals. Do you know cattle?"

Carson shook his head. "Not really. We had a milk cow."

Her eyes sparkled as she laughed. "Oh, Deputy. These Texas brush country cows are nothing like a gentle milk cow. They're flightier than a whitetail deer and just as likely to turn and run all the way back to the hill country they came from."

"Still," he said, "I'd like to ask a few questions."

She glanced toward the window. "By all means. Ask away."

He paused to gather his thoughts.

"Where did you grow up?" she asked before he could speak.

"Not far from Oak Bower, Arkansas." This was not going the way he planned. He straightened in his chair and was about to get to his questions when Marty opened the door and backed into the little office. He carried a tray with a steaming teapot, three fired mugs, a pitcher of cream, and a jar of honey.

While they poured and stirred, Carson mulled over the questions he had for her. As she took her first sip, he asked, "Did you know the Burnetts?"

"Oh my," she said. "I was so hoping for the Major's special tea. Did you know his father buys it from a Dutch merchant and has it shipped all the way here?"

Marty blushed and reached for the tray. "I'm sorry, miss. I didn't know that's what y'all wanted."

She placed her hand on the back of his, and his cheeks turned even redder.

"Never mind. This is just fine. At least with the honey and cream." She turned back toward Carson. "I'm sorry. You were about to ask me something."

"Did you know the farm couple, the Burnetts?"

She shook her head. "Not really. I mean, I met them." Again, she glanced out the window. "I thought it would be so nice to have a woman around, but they were standoffish, or maybe just so busy getting settled, then expanding. Seemed like they wanted to plow up the whole prairie. Well, that and I guess we're always so busy at the ranch, we never got a chance to get well acquainted."

The baby's cries sounded through the door.

Patricia set down her mug. "Oh, my. She doesn't sound happy. I'd best go and tend to her."

"Please wait," Carson said. "I'm sure Bella has everything in hand."

Patricia smiled and stepped to the door. "I've imposed on the poor girl enough. Especially given all she's been through."

Carson said, "Come back as soon as you're done," then watched as she disappeared through the door. He turned to Marty. "What do you think?"

"Pretty," Marty said with a grin. "Smells nice too."

Carson grimaced. "Do you think she or her men had anything to do with that village?"

Marty shrugged. "To me, it's pretty clear the Burnetts did it. Where else would they get all those scalps?"

Carson rubbed his eyes. "My question is why?"

Marty raised his shoulders. "Maybe we should see if we can track down their kin. Maybe they've got a reason for hating redskins."

Gate burst into the foyer and spotted them through the open door. "Come on."

Carson frowned. "Where and why?"

Gate stepped forward. "The major sent me to find you. You'll want to hear this."

"Is it urgent?" Carson asked. "I'd like to talk to Miss Grimwald before she leaves."

Gate scowled. "Around here, when the major barks, you'd best tuck your tail and come a runnin'."

Carson turned to Marty. "You go. I'll wait for her to finish with the baby."

"He wants you both."

As they left the building, Carson spoke to the adjutant. "Would you ask Miss Grimwald to wait for me?"

Gate took long strides, forcing them to trot to keep up. He led them into the trading post and past shelves lined with pots and pans, bolts of red and blue cloth, and canned food. He paused at a closed door and knocked.

"Enter," Major Kinsey said.

A tall, hawk-nosed, gray-haired man sat at the large kitchen table, holding his face in his hands.

Major Kinsey stood near the window. "This is Deputy Kettle and Deputy Dunnegan. Tell them what you just told me."

Without raising his eyes from the well-worn tabletop, the old man said. "It weren't my fault. They snuck in and out without a sound."

Carson cocked his head. "Who did? Where?"

"Must have been the young bucks from the Comanche village. They're the only ones woulda got all thirty head without waking me."

Carson glanced at Major Kinsey.

"Horses," the Major said. "George here was tending a herd of cavalry mounts out west."

"Why do you think it was Comanches?" Carson asked.

George glanced up. "Who else?"

Major Kinsey stepped away from the window. "We settled a large group of Comanche a little further west and north of where we had the horses. They've been peaceful, up to now."

"Do you want us to go after the horses?" Carson asked.

Major Kinsey shook his head. "I've sent Sergeant Buckley and twenty troopers to find out. They're saddling as we speak. I fear this is a result of what's been going on."

"Do you want us to go with them?" Carson asked.

"I want you to find out who has been killing and scalping these people and why. Take Gate and see what you can find at the Burnetts' farm, and talk to the other farmers along the river."

Marty looked from Major Kinsey to Carson. "I thought they found the scalps at the Burnetts'."

The major looked from Marty to Carson, but before he could speak, Carson said, "Something doesn't seem right about that. Why would they do it?"

"Don't some folks just hate?" Marty asked.

"And where would they get the money to pay bounties? There can't be much cash money on a little farm all the way out here," Carson said.

Major Kinsey nodded. "My thoughts exactly."

On the walk to the barracks to gather their gear, Carson's thoughts swirled. He needed to talk to the little boy. Was that why Patricia kept avoiding his questions, or was she just scattered like that? Would Bella be safe here? Would anyone talk to her? Help her? Had the Burnetts paid the buffalo hunters to gather scalps? And if so, why? Who else stood to profit from an Indian uprising? Maybe he should tell

Major Kinsey he wanted to, needed to, stay at the fort. He turned to Gate. "Who would profit from a war with the Indians?"

Gate grunted and walked on without looking over. "Best ask the major. I just do what he tells me and today he tells me to lead you two boys out to Burnetts."

"Did you know them?"

Gate nodded. "Met them."

"And?"

"A little standoffish but seemed like honest folks."

Carson scratched his chin. That was the same thing Patricia had said. Did they have something to hide?

As they rode south toward the Red River and Texas, Marty chattered about the grass and the deer on the hillside and anything else that caught his eye, but Carson barely heard him.

Three hours later, they topped the rise overlooking the Burnett's farm. Beyond the burned-out husk of the cabin, two red-dirt mounds marked the graves of the young couple. Beyond the graves, two big red draft mules and a yellow milk cow grazed in a half-grown field of wheat. Far to the west, a tendril of smoke rose from beyond the next line of low hills.

Carson pushed the sorrel up beside Gate's gray. "Wouldn't any Indian raiders take the mules and the cow?"

Gate nodded.

"Do you think...?"

"I told you, they pay me to guide and track. You're the one supposed to think."

"But, what's your take on all this?"

Gate touched his heels to his mount and galloped down the hill toward the farm.

CHAPTER fifteen

Death and decay assaulted Carson's nose as they stepped into the little barn. His eyes watered, and he cupped his hand over his nose and choked back the sharp, bitter bile rising in his throat. He threw the door wide open and stepped inside. A million flies buzzed and rose as one from a stinking mass of hair and gore, sitting beside a half-finished wooden cradle on a small workbench along the far wall. Above the workbench, tufts of black hair and dried flesh hung from nails.

Marty gagged and turned back toward the door. "Let's let it air out a minute."

Gate brushed by Carson, pulled out his knife, and separated the eight rotting scalps from their pile on the bench.

"Why?" Carson asked, giving voice to his previous question. "And where would they get the money to pay someone? I know farming and this doesn't look like a rich operation."

Without answering, Gate shook a scalp from the end of his knife and left the barn.

Carson turned to Marty, standing outside the door, peering in. "Get in here and help me search.

Let's see if we can find anything that might help us figure this out."

Marty stepped in, then backed out. "I can't. I'll lose my breakfast."

Carson grabbed a shovel hanging upside down from two nails in the wall and tossed it to Marty. "Go dig a hole beside those graves." Once Marty left, he used a pitchfork to drop the scalps into the wooden milk pail he found.

As he carried the scalps toward the graves, Gate stopped him. "Don't reckon you should bury those heathen scalps with those good Christian farmers."

Carson paused. Bella's silky black hair popped into his mind. Blood rushed to his hands and face as an unholy rage filled him. He bit his tongue and, without a word, bumped by the older man. Then he paused and took a deep breath before saying, "We don't know these were heathens. We know nothing about them. And, far as I can tell, the Burnetts are beyond caring."

Once they'd buried the scalps, Carson and Marty searched the barn and dug through the remains of the burnt-out cabin, while Gate smoked and stared out across the prairie.

An hour later, they loped west toward the next homestead. A two-track trail led them between low, oak-covered hills. As they broke into the clearing beyond the hills, two gangly half-grown boys ducked into the small barn. A hard-eyed, black-bearded man stepped from the porch and into the cabin.

Carson stopped. "Hold up here, men."

The bearded man leaned into the open doorway, a Spencer in his hands. He cupped one hand over his eyes. "That you, Gate Rudd? Who you got with you?"

Gate rode ahead a few strides. "Deputies, sent out from Fort Smith."

The man raised the Spencer. "Turn around and ride away, Gate Rudd. And take your trash with you. I ain't going without a fight."

Carson turned to Gate. "Who is he?"

"Name I know him by's Elias Smith."

Carson scanned his memory for a wanted poster in the name of Elias Smith but came up empty.

"Must be wanted for something," Marty said. "We should take him in."

A shotgun appeared from one of the two open windows on the front of the cabin.

Carson stepped the sorrel one step ahead and shouted, "We're not here for you. We don't even know who you are. We're here to find out who killed the Burnetts and why."

Elias glanced back into the cabin, spoke a few words, and shouted back, "Ride in, if'n you must, but I won't leave my missus and my boys alone out here." He turned toward the barn. "You boys kill these men, if'n they try to take me." He looked at Gate. "You know my boys can shoot."

Carson raised the reins in his left hand and the open palm of his right. "You have my word. We just want to talk."

As they passed the low, sod-roofed barn, rifle barrels, one from each side of the doorway, followed them.

Carson held his hands away from his weapons and nodded toward the barn. This was a touchy, cautious family. Was it because Elias was wanted or because of the murder of their neighbors? Probably both.

Elias stepped out onto the covered porch, built of flat stones dug into the red clay. He glanced at the barn. "You boys stay there. They try to take me, kill them all."

"Yes, Pa," two voices shouted in unison.

Elias turned back to Carson and the others. "I won't go with you peaceful. I killed two men, and they needed killing. Now, I just want to be left alone." He held out his calloused and cracked hands. "These ain't the hands of an outlaw."

Carson met the older man's fierce, dark eyes. "We're not here for you. We're here to stop a war."

Elias nodded toward a corral and wooden trough near the barn. "Light, and water your horses. Tie 'em up over yonder in the shade of that oak. I'll have Agnes heat up the coffee."

The horses watered and tied to the hitching rail near the huge old oak tree, Carson led the way to the cabin. A steaming tin cup of coffee sat on each of three stumps against the squared logs of the tiny cabin.

Carson blew over his coffee while he thought of the questions he should ask. "What can you tell us about the Burnetts?"

"Lotta things," Elias said, swirling his coffee in his mug. "Get to it. What do you want to know?"

"How long have you known them?"

"Since we been here."

"Know them well?"

"I suppose."

Carson changed tack. "Any trouble with Indians out here. I mean, before the Burnetts got killed."

Elias glanced from Carson to Gate and back. "Not before, not then, not since. Leastwise, other than when the government forgets to feed 'em."

"What about the Burnetts?"

"No trouble with them either," Elias said. He winked at Gate. "Unlike some. Knew how to mind their own business."

"I meant did the Burnetts have any Indian trouble," Carson said.

Elias again glanced at Gate, then shook his head.

Carson leaned in. "I'm just trying to figure out why the Indians would kill the Burnetts and not come here."

Elias sat back and again moved his eyes from Carson to Gate. He scratched his beard. "You should talk to these greenhorns, Gate Rudd."

The corners of Gate's mouth lifted, but his eyes didn't smile. "The major sent for them. I'm told to show them around, so they can figure things out by their lonesomes. The major don't care what I think, and neither do these boys."

Carson wanted to argue with Gate. He did care, but now was not the time. He turned back to Elias. "What am I missing? Do you know what happened over there?"

Elias tossed the rest of his coffee onto the ground, stood, and said, "I got work to do. Government don't pay me to think either, but I can tell you one thing. Me and mine got plenty of ammunition and we watch. Anyone comes for us, better bring an army." He nodded toward Gate. "Stop by again, Gate."

A few minutes later, the rifle barrels, poking from the doorway to the barn, followed them as they rode west.

Once out of sight of the farm, Carson turned to Gate. "I truly do want to know what you think."

Gate held his eyes on the trail ahead.

Carson's chest tightened. Why was Gate so difficult? He pushed the sorrel until he could look back at the older man. "I didn't want to come out here. There's not much for us here, and I think Marshal Greer just sent us to please the major." He glanced over his other shoulder at Marty. "But after what happened to Bella and her folks, I need to get to the bottom of it. And, I'm sorry if I've offended you. I truly want to know what you think is going on out here."

Gate met Carson's eyes. "Open your eyes and think a little. Should be as plain as the nose on my face."

Carson glanced left and right. A flash of movement on the hill to their north caught his eye. "What's that?"

A bullet thwapped into flesh, at the same time a rifle cracked.

Carson leaned over his sorrel's neck and jammed his heels into the horse's ribs. In one mighty stride, the sorrel streaked full out.

Bullets whizzed past and tore through low brush along the trail.

Carson pulled his pistol and snapped two quick shots toward the gunmen on the hill. As the sorrel hit the trees at the far side of the clearing, he glanced back over each shoulder.

Wide-eyed, Marty hung low over the far side of his mount, as he urged him after the sorrel.

Carson pivoted in the saddle and hauled on the reins.

Gate's big gray sprawled on the ground, facing back the way they'd just come. Gate, his legs under the gray's back, dug beneath himself, struggling to pull his pistol.

Ten painted Comanche braves whooped and hollered and drove their thundering horses down the hill, ducking low branches and dodging brush and small trees.

Carson snapped three more wild shots before clicking on empty.

As one, the warriors ducked low over their mounts and swerved east, then corrected course and homed in on Gate.

"Shoot them!" Carson shouted, as he holstered his Colt and drove the sorrel back toward Gate.

Marty fired. Boom, boom, boom, boom, boom.

The braves veered back toward the east.

Carson jerked the sorrel to a stop beside Gate and reached down.

Gate clawed at the ground, tearing clumps of grass, but the weight of the dead gray horse flopped over his legs, locked him to the earth.

Marty's Winchester barked again, as Carson jerked his own Yellowboy from beneath his right stirrup and leaped to the ground. He snapped a shot toward the warriors, now circling and hanging low over the far side of their mounts.

A bullet kicked up dust not a foot from Carson's own boot. He grabbed Gate's hand and pulled, then dropped to the ground, planted both feet against the haunches of the dead horse, and pushed.

Gate clawed at the earth and dragged himself free.

A bullet whacked into Gate's saddle.

Gate pulled his pistol and snapped a shot toward the Indians, now milling in the cover of the trees on the south side of the clearing.

Carson threw himself over the gray and away from the attackers. As Gate crawled in beside him, Carson rested the Yellowboy over the dead horse's hip, found a red and black painted warrior peeking through the branches of a hickory, and squeezed off a shot.

The warrior jerked and tumbled from his horse, then rolled in behind a clump of low brush. As the downed warrior's horse galloped away, the other warriors disappeared into the trees.

For a moment, everything grew still, even the insects and birds fell quiet. A drop of sweat ran from Carson's hatband and down the bridge of his nose. He swiped it away with the cuff of his sleeve.

Gate crawled over Carson's legs and reached for his own Winchester, still tucked under his stirrup. "Get ready."

Carson took a deep breath and scanned the trees for signs of movement.

A bullet slammed into the gray hide beneath his face. He ducked.

The silence crashed into war whoops. Nine painted horses, one carrying two riders, thundered straight toward them.

Gate's Winchester barked, and the lead warrior rolled off the back of his horse.

Carson settled his front sight on the chest of a wild-eyed warrior, with a red, white, and black painted face, and squeezed.

The warrior tumbled, and Carson settled his front sight on the next screaming, wild-eyed attacker.

Gate's rifle roared. Another warrior threw up his hands and rolled off the back of his horse.

A bullet burned the top of Carson's shoulder. He flinched and his shot flew wild. Behind him, Marty emptied his rifle from the west edge of the clearing. Carson ducked behind the dead gray, touched his shoulder, and felt warm blood. No time to check it now. He popped back up in time to see a smooth-faced Comanche youth swinging at him with the barrel of an old, rusted Spencer. Carson thrust up his own Yellowboy and parried the Comanche's attempt at counting coup.

The barrel of the Yellowboy hit the Spencer and deflected into the warrior's hip and drove him from his horse. The young man rolled to his knees, snatched up his Spencer by the barrel, raised it, and swung it like a club. Carson's bullet took the fierce-eyed young warrior in the chest and rocked him back.

The butt of the swinging Spencer hit flesh with a dull thud.

Without glancing back to check whether the rifle had slammed into Gate or his horse, Carson cast his eyes up, searching for the next threat

Again, the world fell silent.

Carson threw his eyes in all directions. Marty sat his horse, half concealed behind a hickory tree. Two unmounted horses raised their heads and tails and whinnied.

One thundered north into the trees. The other circled, stopped in front of Marty's horse, reached out with his nose, and snorted.

Keeping his eyes glued to the treeline where the loose horse had disappeared, Carson leaned toward Gate. "You alright?"

CHAPTER sixteen

Bella sat alone in the little room the major had provided. Well, not alone. She pressed her nose against baby Perdita, now snuggled in her arms and against her breast, and breathed in the baby's clean scent. She had cared for the baby for the rest of the day, and when Patricia did not reappear, through the night. She left her room long enough to beg for milk and clean rags from the mess hall but spent the rest of the time caring for the little one.

Though she couldn't understand how Patricia could just leave the child without, seemingly, a thought, she was glad she had. Caring for the sweet infant gave her something to think about other than the changes in her body she felt and feared.

Tears formed in the corners of her eyes. One way or another, she would know for sure in the next few days, but something deep inside told her that her regular monthly visit would not arrive.

As her thoughts whirled and swirled deeper and deeper toward total despair, someone knocked on her door.

She pressed her lips together and held her breath.

The person knocked again. "Bella?" a soft voice said through the door.

"Gemma," Bella said, softly. "I'm not feeling well."

The door handle turned.

Bella's chest tightened. It wasn't the children's fault. They didn't deserve any of this. But how could she face them after what had happened to her?

The door swung further into the room.

"Please," Bella said.

A pretty dark-eyed face appeared and Gemma, Phillip's oldest daughter, smiled and ran toward her with outstretched arms. Her three younger sisters followed her through the door.

"Oh Bella," Gemma said. She skidded to a stop just before throwing her arms around Bella. "You have a baby.... Where? Where did you get it?"

The other three sisters gathered around. Liliana, the second oldest, reached out and stroked the baby's head.

For a moment, Bella's heart softened, and she felt a glimmer of hope.

Phillip poked his stern, mustachioed face around the door, then stepped in.

Bella's chest tightened, and the hint of hope that had tickled her heart fled.

"It's time you rejoined us," Phillip said. "The girls need you. I need you." He hesitated. "What I mean is, I can't do anything with them. We can't stay here."

Emilia, Phillip's youngest, pressed a finger to her lips. "Shhh! The baby's sleeping."

Phillip marched into the room, a scowl on his face. He pushed through the children. "You mean you're hiding in your room caring for someone else's child, when these girls need you?"

Blood pounded in Bella's ears, and her face burned. She didn't know whether she was more angry at Phillip or ashamed for not being there for the girls. Taking a deep breath, she whispered, "Patricia Grimwald found her on the prairie. She didn't ask, really, she just left her with me."

Phillip puffed up. "I suggest you give her back. It's time for you to come out and take care of these children. It's time we gather our things and get back on the trail. The summer's wasting away." He turned and marched toward the door, where he turned back. "I suppose with your father gone, we'll have to get married before we leave here."

Married? Bella knew Phillip needed a wife to help him with the children, and she knew he wanted her to fill that role, but with his haughty attitude and stinking breath, he repulsed her. Carson's smiling face flashed across her vision, and just as quickly, her shame flushed his image away. Before she could say anything, Phillip stomped out the door, slamming it behind himself.

As she struggled to gather herself, Perdita opened her eyes, looked from face to face around her, and wailed.

Gemma stepped close. "I bet she's hungry. What do you feed her?"

Bella pointed to the jar of milk on the side table and the cloth beside it. "The trader is looking for a wet-nurse, but I've been feeding her cow's milk."

"Can I feed her?" Gemma asked.

"No!" Emilia said. "It's my turn."

"Let me," Gabriella and Liliana said in unison.

Bella smiled. "Bring me the milk and the handkerchief beside it. I'll show you how I do it."

All four girls ran toward the table, almost knocking it over as they pushed in. Gemma, being the oldest, tallest, and strongest, came away with the jar of milk and held it high above her head. Liliana, the second oldest, grabbed the handkerchief.

Bella dipped her pinky into the jar, then pressed the milk-covered tip against Perdita's lips.

The baby stopped wailing and suckled.

Bella looked at Liliana. "Dip the corner in the milk." She took the dripping handkerchief from the girl and replaced it in the baby's mouth.

One by one, she let the girls dip the cloth into the jar and feed the room-temperature milk to the baby. When the baby turned her head away, Bella said, "I think that's enough for now." She held the baby up and smelled her bottom. "She's wet. I'll show you how to change her."

She unswaddled the infant, then untied the corners of the rabbit skin from around Perdita's legs and bottom. She pulled out the warm, wet cloth and dropped it into a bucket beside the cot. "Bring me another rag," she said, pointing to a neatly folded stack on the single wooden chair.

Again, all four girls darted for the pile, scattering the rags across the floor. This time, Emilia was the first to reach Bella. She thrust her prize out.

Gabriella arrived just behind her and thrust out her own rag. "Take mine."

Bella stroked Gabriella's cheek, then took Emilia's rag. "Next time, I'll use yours."

"That's not fair," Gemma said. "I'm the oldest."

"You can help me tie up this rabbit skin."

Gemma grinned.

"What about me?" Liliana asked, her face red and angry.

"If you're careful, you can take her in your arms and rock her to sleep."

Once Liliana had rocked the baby to sleep, Bella took her and laid her on the blanket she had folded in the corner.

The four girls fidgeted and bumped each other.

Bella felt torn. Part of her wanted to go out with the girls, and another part wanted to stay and hide with the baby. She waved her fingers toward the door. "Come on. Let's go outside, so she can sleep." As the girls filed out, Bella opened the window a crack before following them. Then she led them around to a spot outside the window, where she would be able to hear the baby. "Have you got your strings?"

Each of the girls pulled a knotted string from her pocket.

Gabriella ran to Bella's side and held out her hands with the string wrapped around them.

Emilia bumped her sister. "I want to play with Bella."

Bella raised her finger to her lips. "Shhh. We don't want to wake Perdita. We'll take turns."

Bella's problems slipped away as she focused on the elaborate patterns she and each of the girls made with the cat's cradle strings. She was about to slip away and check on Perdita.

Her heart sank. The major and Patricia marched up the slight rise toward her. A woman with black braids and a blue cotton dress followed them. The woman had a cradleboard on her back. After only a day with the baby, Bella couldn't imagine just turning her over to a stranger. Yet here they came.

She jumped to her feet and rushed around the building and into her room.

Perdita glanced her way, then returned to sucking on her own fist in her mouth.

Bella wanted to scoop her up and whisk her away, but there was nowhere to go, and Perdita was already hungry after this short time. Patricia obviously didn't care about the child. Maybe she could convince her to let her keep the baby, but how would she feed her? If there was a baby already growing inside her, it would be months before she had milk of her own, and she didn't even know how she would feed herself. At least, not without marrying Phillip.

They knocked.

"Come in," she said, her heart hurting in her chest.

Patricia strode in first, followed by the major and then the Indian woman.

"Good news," Major Kinsey said. "Cadwallader found a nursemaid."

Patricia grinned as she glanced around the room. "Where is she?"

Bella reached into the corner beside the cot.

Perdita began to wail, and Bella bounced her in her arms.

Patricia grimaced. "How do you stand that?"

"She's just hungry," Bella said.

Patricia pointed to the Cheyenne woman standing with her eyes on the floor. "Give the baby to her. Just look at those paps. She's made to nurse her own and two or three more."

Bella touched the Cheyenne woman's arm with one hand and held out Perdita with the other. "Her name's Perdita."

"Per... di... ta," the woman said. She reached out and took the baby.

The woman opened the front of her dress, and without shame, presented her breast to the hungry child.

The major blushed and turned toward the door. "I'll leave you."

Patricia laughed. "I'm coming with you."

Bella asked, "What's her name?"

Patricia laughed and shrugged her shoulders as she stepped from the room. "You'll have to ask her."

Perdita latched on and sucked loudly. Soon frothy milk appeared at the corners of the tiny mouth.

Without looking up from the baby, a faint smile touched the corners of the nursemaid's mouth.

Bella touched Perdita's tiny head, then looked at the woman. "What's your name?"

"They call me Martha."

"She was hungry, Martha."

The woman nodded.

"I fed her cow's milk."

Again, the woman nodded.

"What's your baby's name?"

Without looking up, the woman said, "John. After John the Baptist."

Bella tried to be happy. The woman must be a Christian, and Perdita would thrive on her rich milk. She pointed to the bed. "Please. Sit." As Martha sat on the cot, Bella dropped onto the chair. As her thoughts raced in, she pressed her face into her hands and silently sobbed.

Patricia burst through the door. "Come on. She's had enough. The major says it's time to go."

Bella looked up. "Go where?"

"What's wrong with you?" Patricia asked.

Bells scrubbed the tears from her cheeks. "I'm fine. Can't they stay here?"

Patricia frowned. "Here? Of course not. I don't know what I was thinking. Perdita needs to be with her own kind." She motioned toward the door. "Let's go."

Without looking up, Martha stood and followed Patricia outside.

As the door closed, Bella stood and was about to fall face-first onto the bed. She glanced out the window. A cowboy rode by, his rawhide reata tied to his saddle.

She thought of Phillip's girls. She loved them, but even if Phillip agreed to marry her, he would never forgive her for what had happened to her, and she would never escape the shame. People would find out. Her shame would forever taint the girls. She touched her own belly and certainty filled her. She could not let this demon spawn be born into the world.

Tonight, once everyone was asleep, she would find a rope.

CHAPTER seventeen

Carson kept his eyes on the wavering leaves of the treeline as he fed rounds from his pocket into the throat of his Yellowboy.

Beside him, Gate ran his hands down his legs, then reached up and rubbed his left shoulder. "Nothing broken," he said, his voice quivering. "Least, I don't think so."

Carson glanced at the guide. "Good to hear."

Marty rode up, leading a war-painted bay. "Got a cavalry brand. I guess we know who stole the horses." He looked down at Carson. "You're hit."

Carson brushed his fingers over the bloody spot between his neck and his shoulder. "It's nothing." His sorrel trotted up, sniffed Gate's downed horse, snorted, and trotted a circle before stopping beside Marty.

Gate crawled around his dead horse and began to loosen the cinch.

Carson stood up beside the sorrel, pulled the canteen from his saddle, and held it toward Gate. "Here. Let me do that."

Gate took the canteen and grimaced as he tried to roll up onto his haunches.

"What now?" Marty asked.

"We go after 'em," Gate said.

"Right," Marty said. "We'd best get going. Maybe we can catch them crossing the river."

"Nope," Carson said, looking at Gate. "He's in no shape to ride hard or fight."

Gate narrowed his eyes, but held his tongue and nodded.

Carson took a breath and continued. "We'll go back and warn the Smiths. Elias, or one or both of his boys, can warn the rest of the farmers. I'll drop south and warn the Grimwalds. You two can head straight back and let the major know what's going on out here. It's his job to deal with this bunch. Our job's still to find out who started all this, and why."

Heads on swivels they rode back east, Gate riding the painted bay. As they climbed the low ridge east of the Smith's farm, smoke appeared over the treetops.

"Come on," Carson said. "That's too much smoke for a cook fire."

"Hold your horses, son," Gate said. "If Smith or his boys are still alive, they'll be shooting anything that moves."

Carson nodded and slowed his horse. Just before the top of the rise, he turned from the trail and into the trees and dismounted. "Wait here. I'll sneak up and have a look."

The sod roof of the Smith's barn had already collapsed into a pile of smoking logs and rubble. Other than the drifting smoke, there was no movement, and there were no bodies in the yard.

Carson trotted back to the others and mounted the sorrel. "Barn's burnt. Don't see anyone about. Let's go."

"I'll go first." Gate said. He smiled. "I don't think Smith likes you two."

Before riding into the open, Gate paused his horse. "You boys keep a sharp eye out for those Comanches." He turned toward the cabin and shouted, "Smith! It's Gate Rudd. You in there?"

"That you, Gate?" Elias called from the cabin.

"It's me," Gate replied. "We're riding in."

"Comanches hit us."

"I see that. We're riding in."

As they rode into the yard, Elias stepped out of the house and pointed his rifle at Carson. His boys, both pointing their own rifles, popped out the door, one to either side of their father. Elias shook his head. "You boys ease them hoglegs outta your holsters. Slow and easy. We don't want to shoot you."

"What are you doing?" Carson shouted. "We're deputy marshals. We came here to help you. You won't get away with this."

Elias narrowed his eyes. "I ain't got time to palaver. Drop those pistols. The Comanches sneaked in and took our horses and mules, 'fore they fired our barn. We fought 'em, but they got away and left us afoot, so I guess we'll be needing your mounts."

"We ran into them a few miles west," Gate said. "They're long gone."

Elias nodded toward his boys. "Get their guns, Georgie. Any of them grabs iron, you know what to do."

The younger Smith boy, a youth around fifteen, dark-haired, slight, with angry eyes, stepped up to Marty and slid the pistol from his holster.

"I'm warning you," Carson said. "You do this, you'll never have another day's peace."

Elias met his eyes. "I ain't had a day's peace since my momma birthed me. Now keep them paws of yours off'a that hog leg." He grinned.

Georgie pulled the pistols from Marty and Gate and tucked them into his belt. He slid the Colt from Carson's holster and stepped back.

Elias motioned with his rifle. "You boys step down and line up against the wall. Bertie, take them ponies."

"You won't get away with this," Carson said.

Elias grinned. "With what? Finding some loose horses after the Comanches killed you boys. Did I forget to tell you those two boys I had to kill was deputies, just like y'all?" He turned his eyes on Gate. "Sorry you got mixed up in this, Gate. I always enjoyed your stories, but you know what they say about laying with hound dogs."

Elias took his rifle in both hands, stepped close to Marty, grinned, and slammed the butt into his middle.

As Marty doubled over, Carson reached into his own pocket and came out with the little Remington Derringer he'd carried there since finding it in the outlaw Zeke Crusher's saddle bag, back at the Ultima Thule trading post. He pointed the little pistol toward Georgie, who stood with his old squirrel rifle pointing at Gate. "Drop it!"

Georgie spun toward Carson.

Carson fired. The .41 caliber bullet took the

young man in the chest. As Carson re-cocked the derringer and swung it toward Elias, Gate lunged forward and drove his belt knife into the big man's gut.

A bullet slammed into the cabin wall beyond Carson, only a horse jostling Bertie as he shot, had saved Carson's life. The second bullet from the Derringer hit Bertie in the upper lip and dropped him like a rock.

Mrs. Smith screamed, "No!" and burst from the cabin with her old rabbit-eared shotgun in hand. Marty swung his legs and swept her feet, saving Carson from being torn in two by the twin loads of buckshot. As the lead pellets splattered off the rocks of the porch, Carson threw himself onto the woman and drove her to the ground.

She thrashed and bucked and wailed like the devil himself had her.

Carson fought, with everything he had, to hold her pinned to the ground.

She pulled a pair of scissors from her dress pocket and slashed back, just missing his face.

He grabbed her wrist and slammed it into the stone floor of the porch. The scissors clattered away.

After a moment, she stopped struggling. Her body slumped, and the only movement was the rising and falling of her chest as she sobbed.

With one of his hands, Carson held both of her hands to the ground above her head and swept away the scissors with his other hand. "Stay down," he said as he pushed himself off her back.

Ignoring him, she threw herself onto her husband's still chest and pressed her cheek against his beard.

As the smoke drifted up and away from the barrels of the woman's shotgun, Carson's heart raced from the rush and excitement of the battle. He glanced around and, keeping his eye on the sobbing woman, found his pistol in Georgie's belt. He tugged Marty's and Gate's pistols from beneath the young man.

Still on his hands and knees, gasping for breath, Marty reached up and took his pistol.

Gate pressed a boot heel against Bertie's chest and rolled the young man face up. Then he marched over and kicked Elias Smith's dead body in the ribs. "It didn't have to come to this."

Mrs. Smith's red, wet eyes turned ferocious, and she threw herself, fingernails first, at Gate's legs. "You stuck him like a pig," she shouted.

Carson threw himself back over her shoulders and pinned her to the ground.

Once again, she slumped to the ground and sobbed. "And after all the times you stopped in here and shared a cup of coffee or his jug with him. Damn you Gate Rudd. Damn you straight to Hell."

As the rush of the fight left his body, Carson glanced at the bodies of the three men and felt a deep sense of sadness for the hard woman. He tried to imagine what would become of her. One thing was certain, without her husband and sons, she couldn't stay out here.

CHAPTER eighteen

Mrs. Smith sat in the red dirt beyond the porch, her husband's head in her lap. Though dry-eyed, she looked ten years older than she'd appeared that morning, her face drawn and wrinkled. Beyond her husband's dead body, the bodies of her two teenage sons lay in the shade of the cabin.

Carson pulled a thick stack of folded wanted fliers from the rawhide pouch he kept in his saddlebag and handed them to Gate.

Gate glanced at the fliers but did not reach out to take them.

Carson frowned. "Look through them. If she won't tell us his real name, maybe you can find him."

Gate nodded toward Marty. "You look."

Carson shook his head. "He's going to help me dig the graves."

"I'll dig," Gate said.

"Won't be much good with that shoulder."

Gate rolled the shoulder the Comanche warrior had struck with the butt of his rifle, then looked back at Carson. "I can read sign better than most, but I can't read the words on them papers. I'll dig."

Carson shrugged and handed the fliers to Marty. "See what you can find."

Carson threw shovel full after shovel full of red dirt from the grave he dug.

True to his word, Gate kept pace, the red dirt flying as he thrust the shovel into the hard clay and laid the dirt out in a neat pile.

"This him?" Marty said, thrusting a flier in front of Mrs. Smith.

She glanced at the flier and looked away without a word.

"No beard, but it's gotta be him," Marty said. "Elias Hill. Killed two deputies back in Mississippi." He thrust the flier back in front of the woman. "This him? This your man? Elias Hill? Bank robber and murderer?"

She looked from his boots up his legs until her eyes landed on the wanted poster. Tears again welled in her eyes. She snatched the flier from his hand, crumpled it and tossed it onto the ground.

She turned back and ran her hand through her husband's hair. "Banker never shoulda took his farm. His daddy cleared that land. Fought for it. Farmer without a farm's nothing. Got nothing. No way to feed his family. And them deputies coulda just left well enough alone. That Deputy Orv Dubner knowed Elias since they was schoolboys. He coulda left us be."

Marty smoothed the flier and extended it toward Carson and Gate. "You heard her. This is him. Elias Hill. He's worth $500.00."

Gate rubbed his shoulder as he stared at the poster, then glanced at the grieving woman. "I reckon him and those boys was worth more'n that to her."

Carson slapped his shovel against the pile of dirt he'd built beside the grave. "I told him we weren't here for him, yet he would have killed us for our horses."

"I reckon that's true," Gate said, glancing at the woman, who had gone back to stroking her husband's hair.

"If you'll vouch, we won't have to bring his body in," Carson said. "We can bury him with his boys."

Gate nodded. "I'll vouch."

"Give Marty your shovel."

Two hours later, they wound along the trail through the trees, close to the Burnett's farm. Carson walked, while Mrs. Smith sat astride the sorrel, her hands tied to the saddle horn, and a sack containing a second dress, some underthings, and a leather satchel with a thousand dollars in greenbacks, tied over his saddlebags. Carson had discovered the money when he checked to make sure she had packed nothing she could use for a weapon. For some reason, he hadn't mentioned the currency to Marty or Gate.

At the sound of trotting horses and rattling tack, they faded from the trail and into the trees. Carson checked the load in the chamber of the Yellowboy he carried over one shoulder.

When twenty mounted cavalrymen trotted into view, he lowered the rifle and stepped back into the road.

Sergeant Alf Buckley raised his hand and stopped the procession. "Fancy meeting you boys out here." He looked at Gate and then down at the war-painted bay he rode. He shook his head. "Sorry to see this, Gate. Your gray was a fine horse."

Gate nodded, but said nothing.

Alf looked at Mrs. Smith, then at Gate.

Gate looked at Carson.

Alf turned and met Carson's eyes. "Tell me a story."

Carson detailed everything that had happened, and finished by saying, "We were hoping one of Burnett's mules was still holding around the farm, but now, maybe…"

Alf interrupted. "I'm sorry to leave you afoot, like this, but my orders are clear. Get the horses back and bring in those who took them before they incite the rest. Tell the major what's going on, but first, maybe, ride south and tell Old Man Grimwald. Gate knows the way. It's not too far from Burnett's. Oh, and we did spot two mules north of Burnett's, toward the river."

*****

The mules lifted their heads and flicked their ears as Carson and the others topped a small rise. When Carson held out his hand and tried to approach them, they trotted off toward the river.

Carson looked from Gate to Marty. "Either of you a hand with a rope?"

Both men shook their heads.

Carson dreaded the idea of walking all the way back to the fort. "Ride out and around them, easy like, and see if they'll follow me back to Burnett's."

Carson led the sorrel, glancing back every few strides to make sure the mules followed. When they reached the farmyard, he wrapped the reins around a corral post, slipped into the barn and came out with a half sack of oats he had spotted earlier. He poured a handful of grain in the gate opening of the pine-rail corral, and a larger pile against the back rails. He slid between the rail and backed away.

The mules inched up toward the oats in the gateway and took turns nibbling up the kernels. Once the grain near the gate was gone, they stepped into the corral and dropped their heads and began munching the larger pile.

Carson eased around and shut the gate. He found a saddle, blanket and bridle in the barn and saddled the smaller of the two big mules. "Bring her over," he said to Marty, who stood with Gate and Mrs. Smith in the shade of the barn.

Marty touched Mrs. Smith on the elbow.

She jerked away her arm. "I ain't riding that creature."

Carson led the mule out the gate. "Why not?"

"Mule kicked my pa, when I was a girl. He was never the same. I can't abide the beasts, and I won't ride that one or any other."

Marty grabbed her arm. "I guess you'll ride whatever we put you on. This ain't a Sunday picnic. You tried to kill us. You're our prisoner."

She sank to the ground. "Wouldn't a tried to kill you if y'all hadn't come back to take my Eli."

Marty tugged at her arm. "We came back to warn you."

Carson shook his head. "Let her ride my horse, I'll ride this mule." He pulled on the latigo to tighten the saddle. The skin around the mule's belly tightened and wrinkled and the mule cow-kicked, scraping his sharp hoof across Carson's shin.

Marty and Gate laughed.

"What did I tell you?" Mrs. Smith said.

Marty stepped forward. "Maybe you should try the other one. I don't think this one likes you."

Carson led the mule back into the corral and closed the gate. Stepping to the mule's shoulder, he took another pull on the latigo.

The mule reached around and bit his back.

Carson lurched away, tearing a pinch of skin and shirt from between the mule's teeth. His blood boiled as he swung the reins and drove the mule in a tight circle around himself. After a few minutes chasing the mule sideways and around and around, he paused to catch his breath.

Trying to watch both the mule's mouth and his hind foot, he eased his left foot into the stirrup.

The mule stood, relaxed.

"Easy, boy." He put a little weight in the stirrup, then a little more, pulled himself up, and leaned over the saddle.

The mule rotated his left ear but stood still.

"Guess I just needed to show him who's boss," Carson said as he swung his leg over the saddle and found the right stirrup with his toe. He took up the slack in the reins and touched his heels to the mule's sides.

The mule squealed and leaped forward, kicking his heels out behind him.

Carson threw himself back to keep from flying over the mule's head, caught the saddle horn with one hand, and hauled back on the reins with the other.

The mule squealed again and started around the corral, kicking out his heels with every other stride.

After a few such crow-hopping strides, Carson managed to jerk the beast into an ever-tighter circle until the animal stopped.

Marty wiped a tear from the corner of his laughing eyes, and even Gate smiled.

"Told ya," Mrs. Smith said with a scowl.

Carson took a deep breath and eased a little slack into the reins.

The mule walked off like a child's pony.

Carson turned him left, then right, stopped and started, then rode toward the gate. "Let me out," he said to Marty, "then get her mounted and take her to the fort."

"What are you gonna do?" Marty asked.

Carson turned to Gate. "You strong enough to take a ride?"

Gate nodded.

"How far to Grimwald's?"

CHAPTER nineteen

Bella lay on the bed, staring at the pine-plank ceiling. Her eyes traced the water stains spreading from a dark spot in the wood, like crooked rings from a misshapen bullseye.

Every few minutes, she glanced at the window. As the light grew dimmer and dimmer, fewer and fewer people walked past. It would soon be time—but not yet.

Knock, knock, knock.

She held her breath and tried to sink deep into the mattress.

"Bella?" Gemma said through the door.

Bella's heart hurt. As much as she longed to see Gemma's pretty face, to hold the beautiful girl close, she couldn't bear it. She had to stay strong. She bit her lips together.

"Bella? Are you there?"

She rolled toward the wall and pressed the pillow over her ears.

Even through the pillow, she heard the door latch. She threw off the pillow. "Don't come in, Gemma. I'm not feeling well."

Gemma backed into the room, a tray of food in her hands. "You left your supper on the step."

Bella's heart felt too big for her chest as she met the girl's beautiful brown eyes. She tore her glance away. She had to be strong. "Please.... Please just leave me be. I'm not hungry."

Gemma set the tray on the chair and stepped to the bedside. She reached over, pressed her palm to Bella's forehead, then sat beside her. "You're not warm."

Bella turned away. She wouldn't be able to do what she had to do. Not if Gemma stayed.

The girl stroked her hair. "What's wrong?"

Bella forced back the tears threatening to flood her cheeks. When she tried to speak, her tight throat blocked all sound.

Gemma laid on the bed, spooned her warm body against Bella's back, and stroked her arm.

How had this girl learned such compassion? She was only eleven.

Bella took a deep breath. She must tell Gemma to leave, or she couldn't do what she needed to do..., what she must do.

"The little girls miss you," Gemma said. "We all do. We love you."

"I love you all too," Bella said. Her body jerked as a sob forced itself from her throat. She swallowed. "No matter what happens. Just know that."

Gemma pressed in even closer against Bella's back and continued to stroke her arm. "We know. We just want you back."

The floodgates opened, and the tears and sobs poured out.

Without a word, Gemma, the eleven-year-old girl who had lost so much and seen so much, held her close.

*****

A fly buzzed Bella's face. She swatted at it and reached for the pillow to cover her cheek. As she moved, Gemma, still pressed against her back, sucked in a deep breath, then returned to her rhythmic breathing. Bella opened her eyes. The morning sun beamed through the window and lit dancing flecks of dust in its brightness.

She couldn't do what she'd contemplated. Phillip's girls needed her, and she needed them. It wasn't her fault. And it wasn't the fault of the child she was certain grew within her. She would tell Phillip, and as much as she disliked him, she would marry him and convince him to take this new baby as his own. For the girls..., and for this child inside.

Gemma stirred, then rolled back and set her feet on the floor.

Bella turned toward her. "Thank you for staying with me. You'd better go tell your father where you are. He's probably worried."

"Liliana checked on us. You didn't wake up."

"Is it time for breakfast?" Bella asked. "You must be hungry."

*****

Bella sat across from Phillip at the breakfast table. She watched him shovel in eggs and flapjacks.

Golden strands of egg yolk and butter and honey hung from his mustache.

Emilia snatched a rasher of bacon from Gabriella's plate and stuffed the whole thing into her mouth.

Gabriella shoved her younger sister. "Hey! I wanted that."

Phillip glared at the girls, then wiped his lips with his sleeve, stood, and glared at Bella. "You look after them. You've laid about long enough. I've got things to do if we're going to leave soon."

Bella looked up. "We need to talk."

He frowned and, with a look one might expect to see on a parent scolding a child, shook his head. "Maybe later." He turned and stomped out of the dining hall.

Once the girls had placed their plates in the dirty dish tub, Bella turned to Gemma. "Can you look after your sisters? There's something I need to do."

Liliana puffed up. "I can look after myself."

Bella pulled the girl close. "I know you can. I won't be long."

Emilia, the youngest sister, grabbed Bella's skirt. "Where are you going? I want to come with you."

Bella thought for a moment. "Maybe later. I won't be long. I just want to check on baby Perdita."

All four girls said at once, "I want to come."

Bella smiled. "Not this time, but maybe later if it's all right with Martha and Mr. Cadwallader."

*****

When Bella closed the door to the tiny room at the back of the trading post, Perdita pulled off of

Martha's breast with a pop and turned toward the sound of the closing door. Bella was sure she saw a hint of a smile on the baby's face when the little eyes met her own. The little Wichita boy the soldiers had found stood at the window and, without so much as a glance at Bella, stared outside.

Martha closed her dress and looked at the floor.

"She seems happy," Bella said.

Martha nodded.

"May I hold her?" Bella said, reaching out her arms.

Martha extended the infant toward her.

"Oh, look at you," Bella said, wiping foamy milk from Perdita's lip. She leaned her up over her shoulder and patted her tiny back until the baby let go of the gas in her stomach. Then she pulled the little black-haired head to her shoulder and pressed her lips against it. "What will happen to her? Will you keep her?"

Martha shook her head and glanced at her own baby nestled in a cradle in the corner of the room.

Bella pressed her nose against the silky black hair and breathed in the clean scent. Maternal feelings older than humankind flooded her body, and for a moment, she felt a glimmer of hope. Maybe she could take Perdita and raise her as her own.

"Mr. Cadwallader wants to send her to an orphanage," Martha said.

"An orphanage?"

Martha nodded.

Bella had read about the hard life children faced in orphanages. And of the harder life they often lived when the orphanages sold them into indentured servitude. Still holding Perdita, she rushed out of

Martha's tiny room and knocked on Mr. Cadwallader's door.

"Please enter," Mr. Cadwallader said.

Bella burst through the door. "You can't send her to an orphanage."

"Good morning, Miss Foresti," Mr. Cadwallader said with the hint of a smile. "I can assure thee I can."

"But I've read about orphanages. How could you send this sweet baby to such a place?"

"Would thee have her raised amongst the savages or under the loving care of the Society of Friends? If I can find a good Christian Cherokee family to take her, I will, but failing that, I fully intend to send her to the orphanage in New York."

Without thinking, Bella said, "What if I take her?"

Mr. Cadwallader chuckled. "I can see thine affection for the child, but surely the untimely death of thy father and thy subsequent experiences have clouded thy judgement. It would surely be impossible for me to allow an unmarried woman to take on such a responsibility."

"I could take care of her. I may soon be married, and if not, I have my father's books. I'm educated. I could teach school."

Mr. Cadwallader stood and stepped around the desk. As he moved closer, a hint of apple scented tobacco smoke wafted from his beard. He placed a gentle hand on her shoulder and directed her toward the door. "I believe it best for the child to be with her own kind but come back and see me when thou hast a husband."

CHAPTER twenty

Carson stood in the stirrups and did his best to absorb the bone-jarring, stiff-legged trot of the mule. They came onto one bunch of wary-eyed cattle, then another and another, until the long-horned, speckled cattle dotted the rolling prairie. "Not going to be much grass left, if we don't get some rain."

Gate nodded.

"How much further," Carson asked, his aching legs hoping not far.

"Just over that rise," Gate said, pointing to a low ridge running east and west, about a mile south.

As Carson looked longingly at the ridge and the chance to get off the rough-gaited mule, seven riders topped the rise, and as one, pulled the rifles from their scabbards.

"Touchy," Gate said.

"Can't blame them, with those Comanche on the prod."

"They can see we're not Comanches."

As they rode closer, Carson recognized Britt, Remy, and to his surprise, Patricia dressed in britches, a linen men's shirt, and a short-brimmed sombrero.

Patricia's toothy smile stopped short of her eyes. "Deputy Kettle. Gate. What brings you out here?"

"We came to warn you," Carson said. "A group of Comanche boys stole some cavalry mounts, and they attacked Elias Smith and his family. There's a patrol after them and we think they've gone back across the river, but we wanted to warn you."

Patricia glanced at Britt. A hint of a smile flashed across his face.

Patricia pushed her rifle back into its scabbard and moved her horse close to the mule. She touched Carson's sleeve, then brushed her fingers over the bloody shoulder of his shirt. "Looks like they almost got you too." Her eyes, and she brushed his cheek with the back of her hand. "I'm glad they missed."

Despite her fine features and brilliant smile, Carson felt almost no attraction to the slim young woman.

"All right. You told us," Britt said. "Might as well head back. We can handle a few Comanche."

Carson ignored Britt and looked at Patricia. "I was hoping to meet your father. Is he at home?"

"He ain't seeing visitors since his accident," Britt said.

Patricia glanced at Britt, then turned back to Carson and smiled. "I'm sure he'd want to meet the deputy." She glanced back at Britt. "I'll introduce them. You men go on and check those cattle."

Britt frowned and hesitated a few seconds before touching the brim of his hat and saying. "Yes, ma'am. Your wish is my command." He glanced at Carson and Gate. "Deputy. Gate." He jammed his spurs into his horse and took off across the prairie at a dead run. Remy shook his head as he and the other four cowboys eased their horses into an easy lope.

Patricia reined her horse back the way she'd just come. "Don't mind Britt. He's like a spoiled child. He doesn't like to be told what to do."

As they rode up to the sprawling ranch house, a man in an open cupola on top of the house shouted down. Before Carson could comment on the guard on the roof, a gray-haired man in a wheelchair spoke to the black woman standing near him. She took the handles and rolled him into the house.

Carson was about to ask if that was Patricia's father, when she said, "That mule looks a little uncomfortable to ride."

Carson smiled and nodded. "Yes, he is!"

"He looks like he'd pull. Would you trade him for a cow pony?" Patricia asked.

"He's not really mine to trade," Carson said. "He belonged to the Burnetts."

"I don't suppose they much care what you do with him then."

"I don't suppose," Carson said. "He's got a mean streak."

Patricia grinned. "Our Jose's got a way with mules."

"I would appreciate the use of a pony," Carson said. "I let Mrs. Smith ride my sorrel back to the fort."

"Fine," Patricia said. "Come morning, I'll have Jose catch you up a good mount."

Morning? Was she suggesting they spend the night? Her father didn't appear too welcoming. "I thought we might start back after we meet your father," Carson said.

"Nonsense," she said. "It's almost suppertime. You'll spend the night. I insist."

Carson couldn't think of a good reason to refuse, so he said, "If it's fine with your father, it's fine with us."

Beyond Patricia's shoulder, Gate grinned.

Hats in hand, Carson and Gate stood and waited in a large sitting area inside the front door. The smell of roasting meat and fresh bread floated in the air. Carson's mouth filled with saliva and he could almost taste the succulent beef and warm bread the smells brought to his imagination.

Patricia whispered from beyond the wall and a man—her father?—whispered back.

Carson strained to hear, but failed to make out the words.

After more than a few minutes, wheels sounded as they rolled across the wood-plank floor. A tall, white-maned, stern-faced man wheeled himself through the door. His upper body still showed great physical strength, but his legs hung limp and lifeless on the pedals of the chair.

Patricia followed him into the room. "Daddy, you know Gate. That handsome young man is Deputy United States Marshal Carson Kettle." She smiled at Carson. "Deputy, this is my father, Warren Grimwald." She turned toward the doorway behind her. "Please excuse me. I'll leave you to get acquainted."

Mr. Grimwald rolled closer and held out a hand. "I'd stand, but my blasted legs don't work. Horse rolled on me."

"Pleased to meet you, sir," Carson said.

The old man's grip was as firm and strong as any

Carson had ever felt, but while there was no warmth, there was also no hint of an attempt at dominance.

Mr. Grimwald turned and nodded to Gate. "Nice to see you again. Did Jose take your horses?"

"Yes, sir," Gate said.

Mr. Grimwald turned back to Carson. "You men join us for supper."

Carson glanced toward the sounds of pots and pans banging through the wall. "That's not necessary, sir. We've got supplies, and this visit was unannounced."

"Nonsense," Mr. Grimwald said. "I've already told Bruna to put on a few more potatoes and some beef steaks to go with the roast."

"Her feelings will be hurt if you don't stay. As will mine."

Carson nodded. "Of course, we'll stay. Did Patricia tell you why we've come?"

Mr. Grimwald turned his chair and rolled it toward a low, polished walnut shelf lined with bottles and glasses. "Let's discuss it over a drink." He reached up, poured amber liquid from a crystal decanter into three glasses, handed a glass to Carson and Gate, then raised his own. "To finally driving out the savages and bringing peace to this land."

Carson paused. What did he mean by that? He raised his glass. Peace was always a good thing.

Gate tossed back his whiskey, but Mr. Grimwald swirled his glass and held it to his nose before taking a small sip and holding it on his tongue before swallowing.

Carson held his own glass to his nose and breathed in. He mostly smelled the alcohol, but there was a hint of smoke and oak wood. He took a sip.

Expecting the familiar burn of saloon whiskey. The gentle warmth of the whiskey on his tongue surprised him.

Mr. Grimwald smiled. "What do you think, young man? Does my Kentucky Bourbon pass muster?"

Carson's cheeks warmed as he smiled. "I don't know much about whiskey, sir, but this sure goes down smooth."

"From time to time, I have a barrel brought in from Bourbon County, Kentucky. Spoils a man. Makes it hard to drink the stuff old man Doan serves up at Eagle Crossing."

Carson raised his glass and took another sip.

Patricia returned to the room. Instead of trousers and a linen shirt, she wore an elegant blue gown. Her hair had been swept back and small curls framed her face. Carson caught a whiff of flowers as she poured herself three fingers of the amber liquid, and unlike her father, took a big gulp.

Carson had never seen a woman drink whiskey like that.

Patricia grinned, took another belt, and said, "Don't look so surprised, Deputy. Daddy raised me more like one of his cowboys, than his daughter."

Her father smiled, raised his glass, then took another sip. "Tough as she is, she's even more beautiful, don't you think, Deputy?"

Carson didn't know what to say. She was beautiful, and she also commanded the respect of her men. He nodded. "Yes, sir. As far as I can see, she's both."

Patricia's eyes sparkled as she raised her glass and met Carson's eyes. "Why thank you, kind sir."

An older black woman stepped into the doorway.

Mr. Grimwald looked up. "There's Bruna. Dinner must be ready." He reached for the decanter. "Let me top you gentlemen up, before we go in."

Carson already felt the effects of the whiskey and was about to refuse when Patricia took his glass and handed it to her father.

By the time they had finished the delicious meal of roast beef, potatoes and gravy, and warm bread, Carson's head swam. He touched his nose and felt the slight numbness. The whiskey coursed through his body. But the young woman beside him, laughing and touching his arm as she told tales and drew stories of his life from him, was also part of the intoxication.

Mr. Grimwald nodded to Bruna, waiting by the door from the dining room to the kitchen, then pointed to Carson's glass.

As she reached for the now almost empty decanter, Carson placed his hand over his glass. "Thank you, but no."

Patricia touched his forearm. "Enjoy yourself, Carson. You're among friends." She nodded at Bruna, who took Carson's glass and filled it. Patricia picked up her own glass and stood. She looked at Gate, then her father, and said, "Come on, Carson. Let's take some air on the porch. Leave these old men to talk about history or their gout or something."

Gate frowned, and Carson laughed.

Mr. Grimwald smiled and nodded toward the door. "Go on, then."

Gate pushed back. "I'd best check on our horses."

"Nonsense," Mr. Grimwald said. "Let's you and me take a cigar in the parlor."

*****

Outside on the porch, Carson stepped to the railing and stared up at the Milky Way, sweeping from horizon to horizon and lighting the clear night sky.

Patricia took his arm. "Let's walk a little." She led him around the house to a path leading through a grove of pecan trees and down to a wooden bench perched near a small creek.

She motioned for him to sit, then sat close beside him. "What do you think of this country, Carson?"

"Beautiful," he said. "Still wild and wide open."

She nodded. "It is that. It's a cattleman's paradise." She touched his sleeve. "It's a country for powerful men and women who can keep it that way. Don't you agree?"

Carson thought about Mrs. Smith mourning the loss of her husband and sons, and Mrs. Burnett buried beside her husband in the red clay. "It's hard country. Seems especially hard on women."

"Takes strong men and women to live out here," she said, taking his arm and leaning against him.

The warmth of her body joined the whiskey in stirring his blood.

"This country needs men like you," she said. "I'm sure my father would take you on.... If you ever decided to forget all this deputy marshal nonsense."

He hesitated. What did she mean by nonsense?

"Out here, we take care of our own problems. We hold on to what's ours, and we don't need men with badges to tell us what to do."

Carson turned toward her. "I suppose that's the way it's been, but times are changing. I expect before long there'll be towns and churches and schools out here. I guess it's my job to make it safe for those things."

She frowned. "Do you have someone back in Fort Smith?"

"My family all lives in Oak Bower," he said.

"I mean, someone like me?"

He shook his head.

"My father needs strong men like you."

Bella and her dark eyes, once so vibrant and alive and now so sad, danced into his head. He stood. "It's been a long day. I'd best find my bedroll and call it a night."

She stood with him. "Bedroll? I won't have it. Bruna's already prepared the guest room."

*****

Carson tumbled onto the large, soft bed. Next thing he knew, he awoke, his mouth dry and the big house quiet. He walked to the dresser before the window and poured himself a glass of water from the pitcher standing there. The full moon had risen and lit the yard. With the long bunkhouse across the yard west of the house, a low stable filling the gap to the south and an open-fronted shed on the north, the ranch buildings formed an easy to defend fortress, at least, with enough men.

He crawled into bed and tossed and turned until the moon set, and golden sunlight announced the coming day.

Once again, he climbed out of bed for a drink of water. He rubbed the sleep from his eyes and ground his knuckles into his temples in a futile attempt to stop the pounding.

Britt, Remy, and the others rode into the yard from the north. Either they'd been out all night or had risen very early. Remy and the other four cowboys peeled off toward the barn while Britt rode up to the house and dismounted.

The front door opened. First Britt spoke, then Patricia replied, but Carson could not make out the words.

Britt led his horse across the yard and disappeared into the barn.

Carson washed his face and dressed. Carrying his boots, he tiptoed down the stairs. It was time to leave.

As he approached the front door and pulled his hat from the hatrack, Patricia said, "Up so early?"

His body jerked, and his heart pounded. "Couldn't sleep. I didn't want to wake anyone."

She ran her fingers through her hair. Dressed in a plain cotton dressing gown over her nightgown, she padded across the floor in her bare feet and took the hat from his hands and hung it back on the rack. "Bruna will have breakfast soon. She'd be hurt if you left hungry."

CHAPTER twenty-one

Bella's heart pounded and threatened to burst through her ribs. She found Phillip near the three wagons belonging to their little traveling party. He had the contents of all three wagons scattered on the ground around him. As she approached, he picked up a heavy crate of her father's books and set it on a pile of other crates.

"Good," he said. "You can hand me the things we'll be taking. We'll sell the rest," he said, pointing at the pile where he'd just set the crate of books.

She took a deep breath and looked at the crate. "Surely, you don't think I'd go without my father's books."

He frowned. "With one wagon, we won't have room for anything that's not useful."

She was about to argue, to fight to bring the books, to fight for her right to help him choose what came and what stayed, but instead she said, "We need to talk."

He let out a frustrated sigh. "Talk while you hand me boxes." He sat on the back of her father's wagon, the best of the three, and raised his legs to climb inside.

She shook her head and sat on the crate holding Mrs. Trajetta's fine bone china. "We need to talk now."

With a groan, Phillip dropped his legs off the back of the wagon. "What is it? Have the children done something to displease you? I'll leave them to you unless you need me to discipline them. Spare the rod and all that."

"No. No!" she said. "Nothing like that." She touched her belly and blinked back the tears welling in her eyes. Why couldn't he just be quiet and let her speak?

"What, then?" he asked in a harsh voice.

The courage she'd built up almost left her, but she sucked in another deep breath. "It's.... Well, it's when I was taken."

He dropped to the ground and took one step toward her.

Now she had his attention.

"Poppa! Bella!" Gemma shouted as she raced toward them, followed by her three sisters. "The little Wichita's gone."

Without waiting to hear more, Bella jumped to her feet, hiked up her skirt, and sprinted toward the trading post.

"Bella!" Phillip shouted. "Get back here. We need to load this wagon."

She barely heard him as she rounded the corner and ran into a group of soldiers milling around outside the trading post door. She pushed her way through the men. "Excuse me. Excuse me."

She opened the door and burst through. Mr. Cadwallader stood, grim-faced, talking to the major and his adjutant.

"What have you done?" she asked.

Mr. Cadwallader looked at her, then at the major, then pointed to himself. "What have I done?"

"How could you?"

Mr. Cadwallader held up his hands. "I assure thee, I had nothing to do with this."

"You said to come back when I have a husband."

Mr. Cadwallader furrowed his brow and narrowed his eyes.

A baby wailed in Martha's room.

Bella stopped, looked at the door, then back at Mr. Cadwallader. "Perdita?"

Mr. Cadwallader nodded.

"I thought.... Well, I thought." She brushed by the three men, opened the door to Martha's room, and looked inside.

Martha glanced up from where she bounced baby Perdita against her shoulder and patted the little back.

Bella shut the door and turned to the men. Her cheeks burned with embarrassment. "The children said, the little Wichita was gone, and I thought...."

Grim-faced, the major shook his head. "Not the baby. The little boy."

"The little boy?"

The major nodded.

"He looked so sad," she said. "Could he have run away?"

Mr. Cadwallader shook his head. "He could have, but we don't think so. Martha went to the privy and when she returned, he was gone. She roused me immediately. I heard horses gallop away. We searched, but he was nowhere to be found. Not even among the Wichita camped down by the creek."

"What now?" Bella asked.

The major leaned forward, pain in his eyes. "I'm afraid he's gone. We wouldn't even know where to start looking."

Bella watched the red dust puff up before her feet as she shuffled back to the wagons. "Who would take a little boy? And why?"

"There you are," Phillip said, jerking her from her thoughts. He set the spare axle from one of the other wagons into the back of Bella's father's wagon, then climbed in after it. "Hand me that crate, right there," he said, pointing to a wooden box half-filled with the bottles of wine he liked to drink every night.

As much as she wanted to avoid the conversation, she said, "They took my virtue."

His mouth dropped open.

She hung her head and peeked through her hair.

His mouth slammed shut and his cheeks looked as if they might start on fire.

Her breath caught in her throat as she raised her head and began to speak.

He cut her off. "Why are you still alive? Why didn't you fight?"

Tears poured from her eyes. "I tried.... I fought.... They were too strong."

He turned back to the wagon, dropped his elbows onto the floorboards and his face into his hands.

"Please," she said. "It wasn't my fault. Your girls need me."

He remained silent with his face in his hands, then he stood straight-backed and spoke. "Who knows about this?"

She took a deep breath. None of this was her fault. Why couldn't he see that? She dug deep for the courage to speak. "No one but you." She willed him to look at her, but he kept his back to her. "I fear I'm with child."

He wheeled around and jabbed a finger toward her. His eyes and the cords on either side of his neck bulged. "Leave me! Go look after the children. I won't have them wandering the fort like wild things."

"Phillip. Please."

"Go!" he shouted, spittle flying from his lips. His red eyes met hers. Then he looked away as if he could not stand the sight of her and slammed things into the wagon.

She stumbled up the hill toward the fort. Her cheeks burned and her body trembled with both shame and anger. How had she been so stupid? Her love for the children had blinded her, made her think Phillip might understand. No one would ever understand. Her life, at least as she knew it—as she had dreamed and hoped and prayed it would be—died the day those vile creatures attacked.

*****

"You're it," Liliana shouted with glee as she darted away from little Emilia.

Bella glanced up and saw the girls dancing and laughing across the parade ground at their game of tag.

She glanced left and right, then ducked toward the dining hall.

"Bella," Gabriella shouted. "Come play with us."

At first, she wanted to run to her room. Then

she thought she would tell them she didn't feel well. And that was the truth. Finally, she took a deep breath, smiled, and ran toward them. None of this was their fault. "I'm it!"

The girls scattered like a covey of giggling quail.

She spent the afternoon running and playing with the children. Phillip would come around. He would never understand that none of this was her fault, but he would come around to the fact that he needed someone to look after his girls, and that she was the right person for that job.

When supper time rolled around, she entered the dining hall with the girls and looked over at the corner table where they normally ate.

"I wonder where Papa is," Gemma said. "He's never late for supper."

Bella touched the girl's shoulder. "He was busy packing the wagon. I'm sure he'll be here soon." But he wasn't. Over and over, Bella glanced at the door. By the time the girls had finished eating their dried-apple pie, it was clear he wasn't coming.

"Are you alright?" Liliana asked. "You haven't eaten a thing."

Bella forced a smile. "I guess I'm just not hungry."

"You girls play for a few minutes, then get ready for bed. I'll see if they'll give me a plate of food for your father."

Her thoughts raced as she carried the warm, cloth-covered plate down the hill. She had to convince him that marrying her was the best solution to both of their problems.

She rounded the corner where she'd left Phillip packing the wagon. Amongst a scattering of boxes, farm implements, and furniture, the Trajetta's wagon stood empty behind Phillip's, also empty wagon. Her father's wagon was gone.

She ran to the stables. The Trajetta's team stood in their stalls, munching on hay. Her father's beautiful horses and Phillip's team were gone.

Surely, he had taken them out on a practice run. A test to see if the four horses would work together. She set the still-warm plate on the seat of the Trajetta's wagon and wandered among the things he had deemed too unimportant, too trivial to take: Mrs. Trajetta's china, Gemma's small inlaid wood table that had belonged to his dead wife and her mother and her grandmother before her, but most important to Bella, her father's precious books.

As the sun sank below the horizon, a ribby yellow dog wandered up from the Indian encampment along the creek. "Hungry?" Bella asked, as she scraped the cold food from the plate onto the ground.

Phillip wasn't coming back. He'd left her, but more importantly, he'd left his beautiful daughters.

She glanced up at the evening sky. Dark clouds gathered over the western horizon. She picked up the heavy crate of books and slid it in under the tarp of the Trajetta's wagon, followed by Gemma's table and as many of the crates and tools as she could fit.

By the time the rain hit, her arms and back trembled and ached. But all the most precious items were safely stowed in the wagon. She sat on the wagon tongue and let the icy rain wash the tears from her cheeks. She remembered what Mr. Cadwallader had said about baby Perdita. There was no chance she would ever find a husband now, and that sweet baby would soon be lost to her. She looked skyward and prayed. "Please God, let Cadwallader find her a Christian family."

She clutched her chest. What about Phillip's girls? What would she tell them? More importantly, what would become of them? She cursed Phillip for his cowardice, then she began to form a plan.

CHAPTER twenty-two

Mounted on a good buckskin cow pony, Carson loped north toward the fort. The hooves of the buckskin and the bay Gate rode tore chunks of sod from the ground, dampened by a spotty shower that had passed through this strip of land during the night. Scattered groups of cattle looked up from the sparse grass and watched them pass.

He slowed to a trot and then to a walk to give the horses a breather. When Gate pulled alongside, Carson said, "Do you think they've got anything to do with what's going on out here?"

Gate frowned. "They don't pay me to think."

"You're a man who watches and sees. I want to know what you think."

"I think old Warren would do most anything to keep the farmers off the range. And Patricia, maybe even more. She's telling anyone who'll listen that the land across the river is too good for the tribes. She wants the government to move them west out onto the prairie."

"Why?" Carson asked.

"She says sodbusters will be drawn to that good

land like moths to a flame, and there'll never be peace."

"She's likely right," Carson said.

"Does she strike you as the kind to worry about others," Gate asked.

Carson thought for a minute. "I think she offered me a job."

Gate smiled. "She's a striking woman."

"She is."

"Don't be offended, but I think she offered the same job to the major."

"Britt and Remy rode in early this morning."

"Heard them," Gate said.

"What do you think they were up to?"

Gate shook his head. "Don't know. Like I said, they don't pay me to think." He touched his heels to the bay and broke into a lope.

As they drew close to the Red River, Gate pulled his horse to a stop and dismounted.

Carson turned back and stopped beside him.

Gate squatted and looked at a series of hoofprints in the damp sod.

Carson glanced left and right. "Comanche?"

Gate scratched his chin and stood. He walked a little further west. "I don't think so. These are shod horses. Although those cavalry mounts the braves stole were shod too, I suspect Britt and the others rode through here." He pointed to a single hoofprint, then walked a few strides north and pointed again. "Did you notice the horse Remy was riding?"

"A long-backed pinto. Sorrel and white," Carson said, proud of himself for remembering.

"I mean his gait."

Carson shook his head.

"Well, I think this was him." Gate said as he walked further north. "In fact, I'm sure of it."

Carson dismounted. "How can you be sure? Show me."

Gate spread the grass around a hoof print. "Didn't you watch that horse travel?"

Carson shook his head.

"He twists that right rear, every stride. At least, at a walk and trot. Look at this track, then look at this one."

Carson nodded. "Do you notice how every horse travels?"

Gate shook his head. "That would be too much to remember. I just watch for the ones that have something different."

"Seems funny they'd come this far and ride all night to check on some cattle," Carson said.

Gate pressed his lips together and nodded.

They followed the tracks to the ford in the river. Carson turned to Gate. "Looks like they crossed."

Gate nodded.

Carson was about to ask why, but held his tongue. "I guess we'll see where they went, and maybe then we'll know what they were up to."

Gate nodded. He rode to where the land broke and sloped down to the river. He stopped and glanced all around.

"Why are we stopping?" Carson asked.

"We're vulnerable out in the river," Gate said. "Sitting ducks out there for a good man with a rifle."

Carson looked upstream and downstream and, seeing nothing, was about to start forward. He glanced at Gate.

Gate had his eyes locked on a point downstream and across the river.

"What did you see?" Carson asked.

"Something moved."

"Where?"

"See that big rock?"

Carson nodded.

"In the brush just above it."

Carson narrowed his eyes. "I don't see anything."

Gate looked at Carson's leg. "Take out that Sharps, you make your horse pack around and look through the glass."

Carson did as Gate suggested. He sat in the grass, rested his elbows on his knees, found the big rock in the scope, and followed the bank up until he found the patch of brush. At first, he saw nothing but leaves and twigs, then something black caught his eye as he scanned by. Easing the scope back, he found black hair and a dark-skinned face staring back at them.

He rolled onto his side. "You're right. There's an Indian in that brush. Should I shoot him?"

"What's he doing?"

Carson again found the face through the leaves. "Just watching us."

"Any others?"

"Can't see any."

A hand moved up and pushed back some of the leaves and branches.

"It's the boy," Carson said.

"The boy?"

"The one they had at the Fort. The Wichita boy."

"You sure?" Gate asked. "Let me look."

"I'm sure."

"Come on," Gate said. He stood and led his horse back over the hill, away from the river, mounted, and started east.

"Where we going?" Carson asked.

"To get a closer look. Keep a sharp eye."

Carson's heart thumped against his ribs. His head on a swivel, he followed Gate, until the tracker stopped and tied his horse to a clump of buckbrush. "Bring the Sharps."

This time, they crawled forward to a point, straight across the river from the big rock. Carson again found the boy. From this distance the little face half-filled the lens.

The boy's eyes blinked rapidly as he scanned left and right.

"Come on," Gate said. "I can see from here he's alone."

As they rode down the hill toward the river, the boy ducked deeper into the brush.

"Watch he don't run," Gate said.

They pushed the horses across the rocks and into the water. Here, the river had narrowed, and within a few strides, the horses had to swim.

As they splashed up the north bank, branches cracked as the boy bolted.

Carson pushed the buckskin after him, but the brush soon threatened to drag him from the saddle. He jumped to the ground, tied his pony, and started off in the direction the boy had run. Though branches and thorns ripped at his hands and face, he bulled through.

He burst into the open, just as Gate stepped from his horse, took a few long, quick strides, and scooped the boy off his feet.

The boy kicked and clawed and pounded his lashed-together hands against Gate's chest.

Gate wrapped him in his arms and held on until Carson sprinted over and wrapped up his legs.

"It's all right," Carson said. "We won't hurt you."

The boy continued to thrash.

Gate said a few words Carson couldn't understand, then repeated them. After chanting the same words over and over, the frightened boy relaxed.

*****

The day was fading as they approached the fort from the east, the boy riding in front of Carson on his saddle. "I don't want anyone to know he's here or even alive," Carson said.

"Follow me," Gate said. "I know a place we can hole up until dark." He led the way to a small clearing around a clear spring. A well-used fire ring showed they weren't the first people to use the spot.

Carson gathered some dry wood from the forest around the spring and pulled a can of beans and the last of his biscuits from his saddlebag. "Feed him and see if he'll tell you how he ended up there. I'm going in to tell the major what's happened, and make sure he's got a place where we can hide the boy."

As the sun set, a squall blew through, and cold rain-soaked Carson to the skin. Head down, he rode past the Wichita camp near the creek below the fort and followed the road up the hill and past the stables. Two wagons stood where he'd last seen them, but Bella's father's wagon was gone. His heart jumped. Where was it? She wouldn't leave without even a goodbye. Or would she? He had to see to the boy, then he would find her.

The squall blew on and he wiped the rain from his face. Ahead, on the road to the fort, a lone person plodded along. As he rode closer, there was no mistake. It was Bella. His heartbeat quickened, and he forgot the chill in his fingers. He clucked and pushed the buckskin into a trot. "Bella."

She plodded on without looking up.

"Bella?"

She slowed.

"It's me."

She stopped and turned and glanced up with swollen eyes.

"What's wrong? Where's your wagon?" he asked.

She raised her face as if she were about to speak, then choked back her words, spun around, and ran toward the fort.

"Bella. Wait," he said, before pushing the buckskin into a gallop. He splashed up beside her. "Bella. What's wrong?"

"Leave me alone, Carson."

He stepped from his trotting horse and ran to her side. "Slow down. What's wrong?"

She kept going.

He grabbed her shoulder and gently pulled back.

She slowed, then stopped, then threw her arms around him and pressed her tear-covered cheek into his neck. Her entire body shuddered as she sobbed against him.

He struggled to think of something to say, but without knowing what had upset her, could find no words. He wrapped his arms around her and held her, tentatively at first, then as she leaned in closer, he pulled her against his body with one hand and stroked her hair with the other. He glanced around, worried that someone might see them. He'd never held a woman like this before, but suddenly it felt like the right thing to do, and he leaned in and whispered in her ear. "What's wrong? Please tell me. I'll do whatever I can to fix it."

She stiffened, pushed back, and said, "Thank you for saying that, but there's no fixing my problems." She pulled away. "I need to check on the girls."

He swallowed and bit his lower lip. He didn't know what to do or say. He remembered the boy. "There's something I have to do. It may be late before I get back, but I'll come and see you."

She stepped back until his hands dropped from her shoulders. "Forget about me, Carson Kettle. I'm lost." She turned and dashed through the puddles toward the barracks.

He took a step after her, then stopped. As much as he wanted to run after her. To stop her. He had a sworn duty to find out who was behind the scalpings and to figure out why, and he knew the boy might hold the key to those questions and to stopping a war. He turned toward the major's office.

On top of all she had already endured, something new and terrible had happened to Bella. Of that he had no doubt. Once the boy was safely hidden away. He would find her and do whatever he could to make it right.

An hour later, Major Kinsey sat beside Carson on the seat of Mr. Cadwallader's buckboard, as they bounced east along the moon-lit track. Carson stopped the light team where the creek flowing from the spring crossed the road. "I'll have to walk in from here. It's no more than half a mile. I won't be long."

The major pointed to a small clearing on the far side of the creek. "Pull the team in there, and I'll come with you."

As they approached the clearing, Carson said, "Gate. It's me. I've got the major with me."

Gate, rifle in one hand and the boy's collar in the other, stepped from the trees and into the little clearing where Carson had left them.

Carson led them back to the buckboard. "Tell him to lie in the back," he said to Gate. "We'll cover him with that tarp."

Gate spoke a few words of Wichita to the boy.

The boy shook his head.

Gate said a few more words, and the boy backed up a step.

*****

Carson sat on the back of the buckboard and patted the floorboards beside his hip. "Come on. Sit up here with me."

At first the boy stood frozen in place.

Gate said a few more soft words.

The boy nodded, and Gate picked him up and set him up beside Carson.

As they bounced along the road, Carson slid deeper into the wagon and pulled the boy with him. As they drew close to the fort, he lay back, eased the boy down beside him, and pulled the blanket over them both.

At first the boy held his little body stiff and rigid, but as they bounced along, he softened and rolled closer and closer to Carson.

When the buckboard stopped, Carson jerked awake. Tight against him, the boy, still sound asleep, breathed rhythmically, in and out, in and out.

When Carson slid out from under the blanket, the boy's eyes snapped open and filled with fear.

"It's okay," Carson said, touching the boy's hand. When the boy relaxed, Carson wrapped him in the blanket and carried him through the back door of the trading post and into Martha's room.

The boy ran to Martha and threw himself into her skirts.

Carson knelt on the floor beside him and looked up at Martha. "Ask him if he knows who took him."

Martha said a few words in Wichita.

At first the boy said nothing.

Carson stroked his head. "It's all right."

The boy turned his eyes to Carson and nodded.

CHAPTER twenty-three

P atricia bristled, but held her tongue when Britt brushed his horse past hers as they approached the neat farm perched on a flat table of land above the Big Wichita River.

Though the sun had only been up for a little over two hours, Dick Baker and one of the older boys sawed the ends from a stack of pine poles laid in a sawbuck. Two rifles stood against the large oak tree that shaded the men as they sawed. Dick's wife Ethel and the other four children knelt in a large, green garden patch, plucking weeds from between the plants.

Grim-faced and lips drawn tight, Uncle Cliff rode up beside Patricia. "You sure about this? There ain't no undoing it."

She nodded. "Has to be done. We've got to strike while the iron's hot. Right now, nobody will doubt it's the Comanches."

Cliff nodded. "I suppose you're right about that, but..."

Patricia interrupted. "It's no different from cleaning out a den of prairie wolves. Those pups look cute and cuddly, but they grow up to take what's ours, so we do what we have to do."

A floppy-eared red dog caught sight of them and bayed.

The entire family scattered like a covey of bobwhites.

"Touchy," Britt said, with a smile.

Patricia replied, "Smarter than they look."

Britt stopped his horse, cupped his hands around his mouth, and shouted, "It's Britt Viola and Miss Patricia and some of our boys. We're just out hunting strays. Can we ride in?"

Dick stepped onto the porch, rifle in hand. He pressed his hand to his brow to block the morning sun. "Come on in," he shouted. He turned to the baying hound. "Red. That's enough."

Britt and Patricia led Cliff, Remy, Horace, and two other cowboys into the yard.

The red dog, hackles raised, growled, and bared his teeth from his spot beside Dick Baker's feet.

"Light and set, if you've a mind. I'll have Ethel put on a pot. I apologize. It's chicory root. Been a long while since we been to the trader's."

Patricia pushed her horse forward. "Don't go to any trouble. We've had our morning cup. I suppose you heard what happened to the Burnetts and the Smiths."

Grim-faced, Baker nodded.

"We're missing some cattle. I suppose the Comanche got them and took them north, but we were hoping they might have wandered over here."

Baker shook his head. "Ain't seen no cattle over this way since last fall."

"Don't let us bother you. You go on back to work. We'll just rest our horses a minute and be on our way."

Baker leaned back toward the cabin. "No need for coffee, honey. These folks just gonna rest a minute and ride on." He picked up his rifle and started back toward the poles and his saw. "Come on, Ike."

A young man of fifteen or sixteen stepped from behind the corner of the cabin, an old Enfield in hand. He shyly tipped his hat to Patricia and followed his father.

A red-faced, red-haired woman stepped from the cabin, shielded her eyes from the morning sun, and said, "Y'all sure I can't get you something?"

Patricia forced a smile. "I see you've got a well. Is the water sweet?"

The woman smiled. "Lot better than that gypy ol' river water. Lot cooler too." She leaned into the cabin. "Berty, run draw a bucket of water for these folks."

A young woman, with strawberry blonde hair framing her freckled face beneath a sweat-stained blue bonnet, brushed past her mother and trotted toward the rock-lined well beyond the cabin. She didn't look up until Britt smiled and said, "Good morning to you, Miss Baker."

The young woman glanced their way. "Morning." Then hurried on to the well.

Mrs. Baker leaned into the cabin. "Y'all come on. Those weeds ain't gonna pluck thereselves."

Two young girls and a little boy groaned as they pushed past their mother and headed to the garden.

Mrs. Baker leaned into the cabin and came out with a shotgun before closing the door. "Them Comanche got us jumpy."

Patricia nodded. "Rightly so."

Berty, a wooden pail in one hand and a tin dipper in the other, stopped near Patricia's horse. Keeping her eyes down, she held up the dipper.

Patricia took it and drank. "That is fine water."

Berty looked up and flashed a shy smile.

Britt rode forward and looked the young woman up and down. He smiled and reached for the dipper. After drinking it down, he again looked her over, grinned, and said, "Sweet."

Once all the men had accepted a drink from Berty, Patricia took a deep breath and nodded toward Britt and Uncle Cliff.

Britt rode over to where Mr. Baker and Ike sawed. "What y'all gonna do with them poles," he asked.

Mr. Baker stopped sawing and looked up. "Gonna fence off the fields. Keep the game out."

Britt smiled. "Suppose it'll keep our cattle out too."

Mr. Baker smiled back. "Yes, sir. You know what they say about good fences and good neighbors."

Britt's smile fled, and he pulled his pistol. "We can't have no nesters fencing the range."

Both Mr. Baker and his boy Ike dove for their rifles, leaning against the big oak tree.

Britt shot them both before they reached their weapons.

Uncle Cliff had led the other men to a spot overlooking the sizeable garden. At Britt's first shot, he nodded and Remy, Horace, and the others pulled their pistols and shot Mrs. Baker and her three younger children, then they began stampeding through the garden, tearing up half-grown corn plants and smashing squash under their horse's hooves.

As soon as the men shot, Patricia glanced toward the well, where she'd last seen Berty. The young woman had disappeared. She pointed her drawn pistol toward the trees beyond the cabin and shouted, "Find that oldest girl!"

Britt, a wild grin on his face, shouted, "Come on. I hear her running." He spurred his horse around the cabin and down a trail leading toward the river. Remy, Horace, and the other two cowboys started after him.

A shotgun blast tore through Uncle Cliff and drove him from his saddle.

Mrs. Baker, laying wounded and bleeding, swung her shotgun past Uncle Cliff's horse and brought it to bear on Patricia.

Patricia shot the wife and mother over and over until her pistol clicked empty. Then she leaped from her horse and dropped to the ground beside Cliff.

He looked up. Bright red blood bubbled from his lips.

Patricia pressed the heel of her hand against the gaping hole in the old man's chest.

He put his hand over hers. "I reckon we played hob."

"Don't you die on me," she said. "We'll get you to Doc Jones."

He smiled. "Time for me to pay the piper." He closed his eyes, and his raspy breath stopped.

"No!" she shouted, as she dropped her face against his grizzled old cheek.

Behind her, Britt shouted. "There! She run thataway."

Patricia sat back on her knees and scrubbed the tears from her cheeks. She reached down and closed Uncle Cliff's eyes, before climbing to her feet and pulling her belt knife from its sheath. She dropped to one knee beside Mrs. Baker's body, sliced the ribbon holding on her bonnet, then she grabbed a handful of coarse red hair and scalped the dead woman. She tossed the bloody scalp on the ground beside Uncle Cliff's body, then found the three younger children and skinned the hair from each of them.

"I got her," Britt shouted.

Patricia waited to hear a shot.

Instead, Berty screamed and shouted, "No. Please."

"Hold her down," Britt said.

Patricia ran to her horse, swung on, and galloped toward the sounds of the screaming girl and Britt and the others laughing. She found them in a little clearing.

Horace and Remy each held one of the now naked girl's arms, and the other two cowboys held her legs. Britt stood over her and pulled down his unbuttoned trousers.

Patricia pulled the rifle from under her stirrup leather and jacked in a round.

Britt wheeled around at the sound and thrust out his hand. "Don't," he shouted. "We was just having a little fun."

Patricia glared at him.

"It don't mean nothing," he said.

She shouldered the rifle.

"Please," Britt said.

"Patty. No," Remy shouted.

She moved the rifle from Britt to Remy, then shot the girl in the head. As the gun smoke drifted from the rifle barrel, she said, "Uncle Cliff's dead. Scalp this girl, then use the arrows and burn everything. We've been here too long already."

Britt and the men holding the girl all froze.

"Move!" Patricia said, jacking another round into her rifle. She turned to Britt. "Pull up your britches and come and load Uncle Cliff onto his horse. The rest of you do what I said."

Comanche arrows poked up from the scalped bodies of the Baker family, and kerosene flames licked up the outside of the house and barn. Patricia turned her horse east. "Come on."

"I thought we was gonna wipe out the Ketchie village across the river," Britt said.

Grim-faced, Patricia shook her head. "We're taking Uncle Cliff home."

A half hour later, Britt, riding point, jerked his horse to a stop and held up his hand. Patricia, leading Uncle Cliff's horse, and the others stopped around him. He pointed northeast at a line of cavalrymen trotting toward them along the top of a ridge of high land.

"I don't think they've seen us," Britt said, turning his horse south. "Let's high-tail it."

Patricia glanced over her shoulder. A thick plume of smoke billowed into the sky from the Bakers' farm.

"Come on," she said, starting her horse toward the line of troopers.

"What are you doing?" Britt asked as he caught up to her.

"Just let me do the talking," she said.

She rode to the top of the nearest hill, fired her pistol in the air, and waved her arms.

The cavalrymen all looked her way and stopped their horses. After a moment, they turned and rode to meet them.

As they trotted close, Patricia, trailing Uncle Cliff's horse carrying his body, rode out. She forced false fear onto her face. "Sergeant Buckley. They've killed those good people... and Uncle Cliff."

Sergeant Buckley stopped his troops. "Slow down, Miss Patricia. Who did?"

"Comanches. We were out hunting strays when we heard shooting. By the time we got there, the Bakers were all dead. Well, all dead, but that sweet young Berty. We heard her scream, and Uncle Cliff led the charge to save her."

Sergeant Buckley looked back at Patricia's men.

"They killed him," Patricia said, her face and voice filled with honest pain at the loss of her friend and mentor.

"Where's the girl?" Sergeant Buckley asked.

She dropped her eyes. "We were too late."

"What happened to the Comanche?"

"They ran north. We wanted to go after them. Make them pay. But well, I remembered Major Kinsey telling me to leave them to him. We were just heading to the fort to let y'all know what happened."

Sergeant Buckley touched the brim of his hat. "You did right. I'd appreciate it if you'd ride to the fort and advise the major that we'll be riding north after those killers."

Patricia glanced at the troopers behind the Sergeant. Hopefully, none of them were experienced trackers. Someone like Gate Rudd would know in an instant what she and her men had done. "There's nothing you can do for the Bakers," she said. "You might want to cut across country. I bet you could catch them at the river."

Sergeant Buckley again touched the brim of his hat. "Thank you, Miss Patricia. You could be right, but we'd best look to the bodies, before the coyotes and buzzards get at them."

She wanted to argue, but that might bring suspicion. She nodded. "Of course. We should have thought of that. If you'll loan us a couple of shovels, we'll go back and let you get after those devils."

Sergeant Buckley hesitated, then said, "I don't think the major would forgive me if anything happened to you. You ride to the fort. We'll take care of things out here."

Unhappy, Patricia nodded. "All right then. We'll ride to the fort."

CHAPTER twenty-four

One of the babies in Martha's room mewled. Carson nodded toward the door.

Mr. Cadwallader stepped through the door and into his office and pulled the plain canvas curtains closed before lighting a lantern.

Martha held the fussy baby in one arm and led the boy with her other hand.

Mr. Cadwallader rolled the straight-backed oak chair from behind his large, spotless, and neat wooden desk and motioned for Martha to sit.

Carson squatted in front of the boy, who stood beside the chair, with one hand on Martha's arm. Carson glanced up at Martha. "Ask him if he knows who took him."

She spoke to the boy in soft, soothing tones.

At first, the boy said nothing.

Carson stroked the boy's shoulder, and the boy looked up at Martha. As he spoke, he touched his right eyebrow.

"He says it was the one he pointed to the other day," she said, "and a tall man with a cut above his eye."

"Grimwald's man Horace," Carson said. He racked his brain, then remembered. "Britt has a nasty scab over his right eye."

Major Kinsey's face fell. "The Grimwalds' men.... Why?"

"How did Mrs. Grimwald die?" Carson asked.

Major Kinsey said, "Fever."

"Have they had trouble with the Wichita, before?"

Major Kinsey rubbed his temples with the thumb and fingers of his left hand. "Not that I've heard and not since I've been here."

"It's like they're trying to start a war," Mr. Cadwallader said.

The major stepped to the window, pulled a crack in the curtains, and glanced out into the night. He dropped the canvas and turned back into the room. "Patricia wants me to convince the powers that be to move the Indians further north and west. She said this land is too rich and that we won't be able to keep the settlers away."

"She's probably right," Mr. Cadwallader said." But why would they want to start a war over that?"

Carson's legs cramped, forcing him to stand. "I'm no cattleman, but they've got an awful lot of cattle on a short supply of grass on their side of the river."

"Why indeed," Mr. Cadwallader said. "One of the seven deadly sins...."

Major Kinsey nodded. "Greed. I've been a fool, but why did they take him, then let him go?"

Martha whispered to the boy, and he whispered back. She kept her eyes on the floor. "They threw him in the middle of the river, but he says he's a good swimmer, even with his hands tied."

Major Kinsey started toward the door, then stopped with his hand on the handle. "They must think he's dead, but I'll post guards here, anyway." He looked at Carson. "Let's let these people get some sleep."

A half hour later, Carson, Marty, Gate, and Major Kinsey sat around the major's desk.

"It'll be that Wichita boy's word against two white men. I doubt it'll be enough," Carson said.

"What do you suggest?" Major Kinsey asked.

"I'm not sure," Carson said. "We need to find something other than the boy to prove they wiped out the Wichita village."

Marty shook his head. "How we gonna do that?"

Carson stood. "I need to think on it, but there's something else I need to do first."

Marty stood. "I'll come with you."

Carson shook his head. "It's something I have to do on my own. Get a few hours of sleep and I'll meet you for breakfast."

"You're the boss," Marty said.

Carson nodded and stepped out the door. He was the boss. Marshal Greer had trusted him with this, and he had to find a way to both stop the war and prove it was the Grimwalds who had paid for the scalpings and killed the Wichita. At least if it was them. But first, he would look in on Bella.

He paused and listened outside the door to the room the major had provided her. He looked left, right, and behind himself to ensure no one was around, then drummed his fingertips on the door. "Bella?"

When she didn't answer, he rapped a little louder, this time with his knuckles. "Bella?"

She must be sleeping. He was about to leave when the door opened a crack. Bella, still fully clothed, held her fingers to her lips and slipped outside.

As the door opened, Carson saw Phillip's girls sleeping on blankets on the floor.

Bella closed the door and led the way across the parade ground. She stepped into the shadows beside the dining hall. "Go to bed, Carson. I already told you to forget about me."

"I don't understand. What have I done?"

Moonlight sparkled off the tears on her cheeks. "Nothing. It's not you. It's me. I'm ruined."

He remembered her battered body and the blood on her dress when he and Gate had rescued her from the buffalo hunters. He lifted her chin. "Nothing those animals did to you is your fault. They're all burning in Hell, now."

She met his eyes. "I hope so, but it changes nothing." She pulled his fingers from her cheek with one hand and touched her belly with the other. "I have to go see to the girls."

When she turned, Carson stopped her. "Where's their father? Where's your father's wagon? What's happened?"

She looked as if she might burst into tears, but she sucked in a deep breath and said, "Gone. He's gone."

"Where? When's he coming back?"

"He's gone."

"Why? Why would he leave his girls...? And you?"

She hesitated before saying, "Oh Carson, I fear I'm with child. And I told Phillip. And he packed up and left." Her eyes hardened as she glanced across the parade ground. "How could he leave his sweet girls? What will become of them?"

Carson stood with his mouth open and tried to process what she'd told him. "With child?" His thoughts spun. "I thought you didn't like him?"

She raised one eyebrow, then dropped her eyes. "Not Phillip."

He'd been a fool, but now he understood. Before he could say anything, assure her it still wasn't her fault, she sprinted across the parade ground and slipped back into her room.

He ran after her and tried the door, but she had thrown the bolt. He knocked. "Bella. Please. Come out and talk to me."

A tiny, frightened voice said, "Bella. Someone's knocking. I'm afraid."

"Go back to sleep, little one. It's Deputy Kettle, but he's leaving."

Carson stood outside the door for several minutes, then plodded off to his own room.

He tossed and turned on top of his blanket until Marty tapped on the door. "You ready for breakfast?"

"Go on. I'll be right there." He took a minute to shave his face with cold water and put on his clean shirt. On the way to the dining hall, he stopped outside Bella's door and listened. "Bella?" he whispered.

No one answered, but the bed creaked.

"I've got things I have to do. Marshal things. But we need to talk. Please. Don't decide anything until I get back."

Soldiers on their way to breakfast stared at him, or so it felt. "Please," he said. "Promise you'll wait until I get back."

"Go," Bella whispered. "I'll wait."

*****

Marty, Gate, and Major Kinsey had started their breakfasts by the time Carson sat down.

Major Kinsey's adjutant rushed in. "Remy, from the Grimwald ranch, is in your office, Sir. He says he has an urgent message for you."

The major's face turned red, and his eyes narrowed as he banged down his fork and stood.

"Wait," Carson said. He glanced around the room. Several of the major's men had stopped eating when the adjutant rushed in and now stared at the major's table. Carson leaned across and whispered. "Let's talk outside."

Marty and Gate pushed back from the table.

Carson said, "I think it best if the major and I talk to him alone."

Marty smiled and turned back to his plate. "You're the boss."

Gate just nodded and went back to his remaining egg and slice of bacon.

Major Kinsey nodded and started for the door.

Once they were away from listening ears, Carson said, "We should listen to what he says, but not let on that we know anything. And especially that the boy is still alive, or that we know what Britt and Horace did. Let's just see what he says." He glanced at the major, hoping to get a sign of agreement, but the major was staring toward his office.

"I need more evidence," Carson said, "if we're going to get them before the judge and make them pay."

Major Kinsey turned back to Carson and nodded. "That's wise. I'll let you do the talking."

Carson's legs trembled, and his mind raced as he turned toward the major's office. He wasn't ready to do the talking. He took a deep breath. Ready or not, he was the deputy in charge. He nodded.

Carson and Major Kinsey stepped into the office.

Crimson-faced, Remy turned away from the window beside the adjutant's desk. He wrung his hat in his hands. "Miss Patricia sent me. She wanted to come, but she sent me. Old Cliff got shot...."

"Slow down, Remy," Carson said.

Major Kinsey stepped towards the door to his office. "Let's talk in here." He glanced at the adjutant, now sitting at his desk. "Could you bring us coffee?"

Once in the office, the major sat behind his desk while Carson and Remy sat across from him.

Remy spoke again.

Carson slid his jacket aside, exposing his Deputy Marshal badge, touched Remy's shoulder, and drew his eyes. "Tell us what happened."

Remy's eyes flashed back and forth from Major Kinsey to Carson.

Major Kinsey, sitting with a pencil in hand, locked his eyes on Carson.

Remy shifted in his chair until he mostly faced Carson. He blinked rapidly, then looked up toward the ceiling. "Well. Well, Miss Patricia said...."

Carson leaned in. "It's all right, Remy. Just tell us what happened to Cliff."

Remy swallowed. "He charged off to save that pretty little strawberry blond girl, and Comanches shot him."

"Girl?" Carson asked.

"That Baker girl. We was hunting strays, and we heard some shots. Lots of shooting. We hightailed it over to the Bakers, but we was too late. Then that girl screamed from out there in the woods by the river, and Cliff charged over to save her, but they shot him. Killed him dead."

"I'm sorry to hear that," Carson said. "Where's the girl now?"

"Killed her too."

"Did you see the killers?"

"No, sir. But them folks was all scalped and stuck like pincushions with arrows."

"Did you go after them?"

Again, Remy hesitated and looked up. "No, sir. We feared they was too many."

"Where did they go?"

"North. Sergeant Buckley took off after them."

Now Carson was confused. He glanced at Major Kinsey, who only shrugged. "Sergeant Buckley?" Carson asked.

"He told Miss Patricia to ride over here to tell y'all he went after the savages, but she sent me. She wanted to get Cliff home for burying."

Carson nodded. "Was Sergeant Buckley with you?"

Remy shook his head. "No, sir. We met him on the trail."

Carson looked at Major Kinsey. "Anything else?"

The major glanced down at the notebook where he had recorded Remy's words. He shook his head. "Can't think of anything."

The adjutant knocked, then backed through the door with a tray holding a coffee pot and three cups.

The major gestured toward the table in the

corner, then said, "What was I thinking? I'll bet you've been riding and haven't had a thing to eat." He stood. "Let's go get you some breakfast."

Remy bounced to his feet and almost twisted his hat in two. "Oh no, sir. That's very kind, sir, but I'd best head back for the plantin'. Old Cliff and me, well we worked together long as I can remember, and I'd like to see him off."

The major glanced at Carson, then nodded. "I understand."

"I can have the cook pack you something."

Remy started toward the door. "Oh no, sir. I'd best be on my way."

They followed him out the door and watched him mount his drooping horse and ride south.

Major Kinsey turned to Carson. "What do you think?"

"I think he's lying," Carson said.

The major nodded. "I agree."

Carson sighed. "I still don't think we have enough evidence."

"So, what's the plan now?"

Carson shrugged. "I suppose I'll have to ride out there at some point, but before I go, I'd like to hear what Sergeant Buckley has to say."

The major looked west. "I suppose I could send Gate out to find him, but even if Remy's lying, there's still the matter of the attack on the Smith's and our stolen horses."

"Do you think Gate could even find them?"

"If anyone can," the major said.

Carson glanced toward the dining hall. "Seems like the best plan, then. Marty and I will go with him."

CHAPTER twenty-five

Carson and the major skirted a troop of soldiers marching in order around the hard-packed clay parade square. A sergeant barked commands at the soldiers and ordered them to stop and face the major. Major Kinsey saluted, and the troops saluted back.

As they stepped onto the porch of the dining hall, Phillip's girls spilled out the door. Laughing and scuffling with one another, they ducked and darted between the marching soldiers.

At first, Carson grinned at their exuberance, then he frowned. Either their father had returned, or they didn't yet realize he was likely gone for good.

Bella followed them through the door. She glanced at Carson and the major, then dropped her eyes to the ground and sped up.

"Good morning, Bella," the major said.

She glanced up, but kept walking. "Morning, sir."

"I need to talk to Phillip," Major Kinsey said, "but later. Is he inside?"

She shook her head.

"Oh my. Are you not well?" Major Kinsey asked.

Dark circles cradled Bella's puffy eyes.

She paused mid-stride and glanced at Carson. "I'm fine."

"Ask Phillip to come and see me, please," the major said.

Bella pulled back her shoulders and took a deep breath. "He's gone."

"Gone?" the major asked. "Gone where?"

Bella dropped her eyes to the red clay of the parade ground and shrugged her shoulders.

"When will he be back?"

She glanced at Carson and shrugged again.

Major Kinsey looked from Bella to Carson. "Did you know about this?"

Carson nodded.

"Why didn't you tell me?"

"Not really my affair," he said.

Pain flashed in Bella's eyes.

Carson's chest tightened. "What I mean, sir, is it.... Well, I suppose, I thought Bella would tell you in her own good time."

Major Kinsey glanced toward the children, laughing and playing on a grassy patch beyond the parade ground. "Surely, he'll be back. His children are still here."

Bella raised her eyes. "He took four horses and a wagonload of supplies." Tears welled in her eyes. "He didn't tell me.... He didn't tell his girls he was leaving. I don't think he's coming back."

The major snapped his open mouth shut. "Oh my. We must talk. When I'm done here. I'll come and find you."

Bella glanced at Carson, her eyes filled with pain. "I'll be in my room."

As she walked away, the major said, "I need to talk to Cadwallader about this." He turned and walked into the dining hall.

Marty and Gate sat at the same table. Gate held his coffee cup in both hands and glanced at the door. Marty sat with his back to Gate, laughing and talking with the soldiers at the next table.

The major walked over and looked at Gate. "I need you to take these two out and find Buckley." Then he turned on his heel and marched back out the door.

Mouths open, Marty and Gate looked up at Carson.

Carson said, "Gather enough supplies to hold us until we find Buckley and his men, and saddle my horse. I'll meet you at the stables in half an hour." He turned and headed toward the door.

"What's going on?" Marty asked.

Carson continued walking. "I'll explain later."

He crossed the parade ground to Bella's room and knocked on her door.

"Who is it?" she said.

"It's me."

"Go away."

"Please come out and talk to me."

"Leave me alone."

Why was she doing this? He only wanted to help, though he had no idea what he could or should do to make things better. "Please, Bella. Come out here and talk to me."

"I said leave me alone, Deputy. Go away and mind to your marshal business."

Why was she angry at him? He glanced all around. Seeing no one watching, he tried the door.

When it opened, he ducked inside and closed it behind himself. Bella lay curled on the cot.

She sat up and said, "Get out." Tears spilled over her cheeks as she began to weep. Through the tears, she said, "I don't know what to do."

He sat beside her and wrapped an arm around her. "I don't know what you should do either, but I'll help."

"You can't," she said. "No one can. Phillip's not coming back. I know it. Cadwallader will send the children with Perdita to some orphanage back east. I'll have this child and you know what will become of me. With no family. No friends. There's only one way, I'll be able to feed myself and this baby."

Carson looked at her. "What do you mean?"

"On my back. Up above a saloon."

Carson blinked back his own tears. There had to be another way. None of this was Bella's fault. "Don't say that. Please, don't."

"Now the major knows, he can't let us stay here. He'll send me and the children back to Fort Smith on the next supply run."

"Let me talk to him. I'll go with you. You can all stay with my Ma and Pa until I figure it out."

She shoved him away and stood. "Really, Deputy? Do you really think your family could take on five..." she glanced at her belly, "six more mouths?"

He hesitated, trying to gather his thoughts. This was all coming on so fast.

"See," she growled. "Even you know they couldn't do it."

"I've got money coming from Elias Smith, and I'll get more...."

She turned her back on him. "You're a dreamer. A kind dreamer, but I'll take care of it myself."

"How?"

She scrubbed the tears from her cheeks and turned toward him with hard eyes. "Get on with your marshal duties, Deputy Kettle. Mind your own business and leave me to mind mine."

"I have to go, but I beg you to wait until I come back before you decide anything. I'll ask the major to wait too."

Her eyes narrowed, and her lush lips thinned. "I said mind your own business." She marched to the door and held it open. "Go on, now."

"Just check and make sure no one's watching."

"Doesn't matter if they are. Now go!"

Carson stepped past Bella and out the door, and slammed into Mr. Cadwallader, almost knocking the older man to the ground. "I'm so sorry," Carson said.

Mr. Cadwallader straightened his stiff black jacket and looked from Carson to Bella and back. "Hmmmm," was all he said, but his eyes clearly told the story of what he thought of Carson being in Bella's room, unchaperoned.

"It's not what you think," Carson said.

Mr. Cadwallader face grew even redder as he wagged a finger in front of Carson's face.

Bella stepped back and closed the door.

"Wait," Mr. Cadwallader said. "I was just coming to speak to you, Miss Foresti. Major Kinsey sent me."

Marty and Gate rode around the corner, Marty leading Carson's sorrel. "Ready?" Marty shouted.

Carson glanced at Bella, who had now reopened the door.

Pain and fear twisted her beautiful features. Her red-rimmed eyes met his. "Go on now, Deputy."

Cadwallader turned to Carson. "Yes, please go, and let me speak with the young woman."

After one last look at Bella, Carson turned away and mounted his horse.

Gate led them out past the fort buildings and turned south. "Best we start at Baker's farm."

As they rode along the high ground east of Cashe Creek and toward the Red River, Carson spun his head toward the west. "Wait! What was that?"

"What was what?" Marty asked.

Carson pointed at a ridge a mile or more west. "I think I saw riders coming down the hill on the road west."

"Riders?" Marty asked. "I don't see anyone."

A troop of cavalrymen rode back into view from a low spot in the road.

Gate raised his hand to his eye and peeked through a tiny hole he created by curling his forefinger. He turned his horse back toward the fort. He smiled at Carson. "Looks like you found them." For a second, the corners of his lips rose, and his eyes narrowed. "I bow to your tracking skills, Deputy Kettle."

"What was that?" Marty asked. "Did you just smile?"

"I believe he did," Carson said with a grin.

Gate blew like a horse flapping his lips and started back toward the fort. "Let's go find out what's going on."

A dust-covered trooper, with weary eyes, trotted down the hill toward them. Before Gate or Carson could ask, the cavalryman said, "Oh good. There you are. The major wants to see you."

As they entered the office suite, the major's adjutant looked up and nodded toward the major's door. "Go on in."

Major Kinsey looked up as Carson opened the door. "That was quick. I was afraid you'd be further gone." He looked to Sergeant Buckley. "I guess you'd better start over."

Sergeant Buckley described finding the bodies at the Bakers' homestead. "Something didn't look right about those arrows," he said. "Looked like someone just stuck them in, in a bunch." He looked at Gate. "Wish you'd been with us."

Gate cocked his head as if to ask why.

"You'd a seen right away there weren't no tracks heading north. As it were, we all rode around and messed things, 'til the buzzards led Courts and I to the girl. We were afoot, and I started looking around. I figured I might find some spent cartridges or something. Then Courts said, 'I don't know about this, Sarge. Best I can see there's no tracks, but those that came out here from the house. Wouldn't those Comanche have left their horses nearby?'"

"We made a big circle, and sure enough, there was no horse tracks anywhere north of the farm."

"Could they have gone another way?" Major Kinsey asked.

Sergeant Buckley shook his head. "Both Britt and Patricia said the warriors ran north." He looked at Gate. "We thought maybe they rode down into the Big Wichita, but we followed the banks all the way to the Red and never saw any sign that anyone had come out of the river, nor crossed the Red."

"Good work, Sergeant," Major Kinsey said. "Feed your men and tell them to get some rest. I believe we'll be riding south soon."

After Sergeant Buckley left, Carson said, "I think I still need more evidence."

Gate slammed his hand on the desk. "More?" He glanced at the major. "Sorry, sir."

The major waved toward Gate as if to say, no problem. "I believe we may have enough from a military point of view to charge them with fomenting insurrection, but I agree that the murder charges should be handled by a civilian judge. What more do you think you need?"

Carson thought for a moment. "We have the boy who can testify to them wiping out the Wichita village, but I'm not sure that's enough to see them hanged. We've got circumstantial evidence they killed the Bakers, but I want evidence they killed white people and paid for scalps. Bella needs justice for her father and their friends. We need an admission."

Marty shook his head. "How are we going to get that?"

Carson looked at each of the men. "Give me an hour to think. I've got an idea."

CHAPTER twenty-six

Carson sat on the hard, straight-backed wooden chair in the little room the major had provided for him and Marty. He licked the lead of the pencil and began to write. Unhappy with the words, he crumpled the paper and shoved it to one side of the little wooden table. Taking a clean sheet, he started again.

Dearest Mother and Father,

I am about to embark on a dangerous mission. One I hope will bring a group of heinous murderers to justice.

Though I have every confidence I will succeed, should this letter reach you, I have failed and will not return.

I have a favor to ask.

My dear friend, Miss Bella Foresti, through no fault of her own, finds herself in dire circumstances. In addition to her personal problems, and as a testament to her stellar character, she loves, and has taken charge of, four orphaned girls.

As I am now unable to see to them, I beseech you to take my share of the reward money for one Elias Hill, otherwise known as Elias Smith, and use it to help Miss Foresti and the children start a new life together.

He paused and tapped the pencil against the side of his head, then continued writing.

It will become apparent that Miss Foresti is with child. This is the result of her abduction and despoilment by evil murderers. I know you taught me never to lie, but I beg of you to, for this good woman's sake, say that the child is mine and that we were married prior to my death.

Miss Foresti is an educated woman who loves children and would make an excellent teacher.
Thank you for this.
Your loving son,
Carson

He folded the letter and sealed it in an envelope, then wrote a second letter to Bella, telling her what he'd done. He wrote a third letter to Major Kinsey, asking that he allow Bella and the children to travel to Oak Bower to live under the care and guidance of his parents on their farm.

He gave all three letters to Major Kinsey on condition that he only open his own letter and deliver the other two in the event of Carson's death.

After leaving the major's office, Carson stopped by Bella's room and knocked. When there was no answer, he crossed the parade ground to the dining hall, where he found Marty sharing a story with Gate and Sergeant Buckley.

He met Marty's eyes. "Excuse me gentlemen, but I need a word with the deputy in private."

When Marty joined him outside, he unpinned his badge and handed it over.

Marty took it and stuffed it in his trousers. "You sure about this?"

Carson nodded. "There's one more thing. If anything happens to me..."

"Don't even say that."

"I mean it. I need you to take Bella and the girls to my parent's farm. Major Kinsey will give you a letter for them. And I need you to convince Marshal Greer to give Bella my share of the reward for Elias."

Marty was about to speak when Carson squeezed his arm. "Promise me."

Marty nodded, his face drawn and solemn. "I promise. If she needs it, she can have my share too. Be careful out there."

"I will," Carson said. He smiled and found Marty's eyes. "If I'm not back in four days, I expect to see you leading the cavalry charge to save me."

*****

After a long and lonely ride, Carson took a deep breath and steadied his trembling hands, as he rode into the compound on the Grimwald's ranch.

Having been warned by the guard in the cupola, Patricia and her father waited on the porch.

Patricia forced her tight lips into a smile. "What brings you all the way out here, Deputy Kettle?"

Carson smiled and touched the two pinholes in his shirt. "I guess it's just Carson now."

Patricia hesitated. "You mean...?"

Carson nodded. "I decided I'd be better off making my own way in the world. I'd like to go west and start my own ranch, but I admit, I know little of cattle. I was hoping your offer still stood, and that maybe I could spend a season or two here learning to be a rancher."

Now Patricia genuinely smiled. "Of course, it does." She looked at her father. "I told Carson you would hire him." When her father frowned, she said, "Truth be told, I said you might hire him. He might not know cattle, but he rode into the territories and drug out old Lijah Penne by the ear."

The old man nodded. "I heard about that. Throw your things in the bunkhouse. I'll have Jose set you up."

Patricia touched her father's shoulder. "Why don't we let him stay in the guest room. At least until he gets settled."

Mr. Grimwald looked up at his daughter, paused a few seconds, and shook his head. He looked at Carson and smiled. "You'll learn. There's no use arguing with her. Put your horse away and bring your things into the house."

*****

Carson sat on the soft bed and mulled over and over the stories he planned to spin.

A knock on the door snapped him back to the moment.

"Suppertime," Patricia said.

"I'll be right down," Carson said. He buttoned and tucked in his shirt, looked in the little mirror over the dresser, and ran his fingers through his hair. He took a deep breath and forced a smile.

To his surprise, Patricia waited for him in the hallway. Dressed in a beautiful yellow dress, with her hair in curls around her face, she smiled and took his arm.

As they came down the stairs into the living room, her father and Britt looked up. Britt's eyes narrowed and turned dark. Mr. Grimwald smiled. "There you are. I think you met our foreman, Britt."

"Yes, sir," Carson said.

"He'll be joining us for dinner."

"Delightful," Patricia said, though her tone suggested she felt otherwise.

Patricia kept up a stream of chatter through dinner. For his part, Carson smiled and nodded and answered Patricia's questions. She asked a little about his raising, but mostly, she wanted to know about his bringing in Lijah Penne. Every time he spoke of shooting or killing, she smiled and glanced at her father.

Mr. Grimwald glanced up from time to time but said little.

Britt bolted his food without looking up. When he finished eating, he glared from Carson to Patricia to Mr. Grimwald. "I won't have him treated special. He wants to learn to ranch. He'll sleep and eat with the men."

Patricia's eyes hardened. "That's not for you to say. Last I knew, you were still an employee."

Britt sucked in a deep breath and appeared about to speak, when Mr. Grimwald said, "Come and see me tomorrow, Britt. We'll discuss it."

Britt looked at the older man. "But you said..."

"Tomorrow," Mr. Grimwald said.

Britt nodded and stormed out.

"Well," Patricia said, "That was pleasant."

Carson looked at her. "I don't mind sleeping in the bunkhouse."

She turned her hard eyes on him. "As long as you work here, you'll sleep where I tell you." Her face softened, and she looked at her father. "Or where Daddy tells you."

Mr. Grimwald looked at Carson and smiled. "Remember what I told you about my girl. She's a lot like her mother."

Carson smiled. "I'll remember, sir."

Mr. Grimwald. Set down his fork. "I see you carry a Sharps."

"Yes, sir," Carson said.

"You any good with it?"

"Yes, sir."

Mr. Grimwald smiled. "That's good. We got a lot of varmints on our range. You got lots of ammunition for it?"

"Just one box."

"Put a case on the list Patty."

"That's an awful lot," Carson said.

"Patty likes you. You prove yourself to me, we could keep you around a good long time, and like I said, we got a lot of varmints."

"Wolves?" Carson asked, fishing for details but wanting to slow play his questions.

"Those too," Mr. Grimwald said with a grin. He rolled his chair back from the table and yawned. "I'm not the man I once was," he said. "I'll bid you goodnight. Patty can fill you in on things around here. She knows as much or more as I do about what goes on, but don't stay up too late. The men eat at six and they're working by six thirty."

"Thank you, sir, and good night," Carson said. "I should call it a night too." He rose.

Just as he'd hoped, Patricia placed a firm hand on his shoulder. "Not so fast Carson Kettle. You and I are going to have a drink before retiring."

Mr. Grimwald looked at them, then smiled. "I'll make sure Bruna keeps an eye on you." He winked. "For your protection, Mr. Kettle."

Patricia poured three fingers of her father's fine whiskey into each of two glasses. She handed one to Carson. "It's a beautiful evening. Let's step outside."

Carson smiled and nodded.

They stood on the porch, sipped their drinks, and gazed at the night sky. Patricia set her drink on the railing. "I love this place, but it's under attack. If we don't fight for it, we'll lose it piece by piece."

"What do you mean?" Carson asked.

She waved her hand from horizon to horizon. "Most of this is open range. We're filing on as much land as we can. We've even got the hired hands filing on all the good water holes, but with so much fertile bottomland along the rivers, we can't keep the nesters out."

"I'm willing to file on a plot if you need me to," Carson said.

She smiled. "Finish your drink. I want to show you something. Let's walk." She took his arm and led him along a different path to the grove of pecan trees planted beside the creek. She pointed to a white cross in a little plot, fenced with white pickets. "That fresh grave is Uncle Cliff. That big cross is my momma. She planted these pecans. That's how long we've been here. Daddy and Momma and Uncle Cliff fought off the Comanche and all the others. This is all our land, no matter what the government says." She pulled him along the trail to the little bench beside the creek.

Instead of sitting, she turned and pulled his body against hers.

Carson's breathing stopped, and his heart thumped in his chest. He'd never been this close to a woman, except maybe his mother. And this was different, much different.

She pressed his cheeks between her warm hands and her lips to his.

Her sweet floral perfume filled his nose, and the heat of her body melded with the fire building in his.

She leaned back and pulled her lips from his. "Have you never kissed a girl?"

He shook his head.

"Close your eyes."

When he did, she again pressed her lips to his. He wasn't sure what to think when her mouth opened and her tongue pressed against his lips. At first, he squeezed his lips tight, but her gently probing tongue soon found its way past his teeth and flickered across his own tongue.

Soon, waves of energy flowed up and down his body, and his tongue, as if it had a mind of its own, matched hers.

She pulled back. "Did you like that?"

He thought of Bella, and a wave of guilt flashed through him, but he nodded.

"I need you to do something for me."

"What?"

"We'll it's Britt. He thinks he owns me. He thinks he owns this ranch."

"Why don't you fire him?"

"My father likes him. He's a good man in a fight and there's no job too low or too dirty for him."

"What could I do?"

She took his wrist and placed his open palm on her breast.

He tried to pull his hand away, but she held on and pressed it against her dress. "I need you to use your Sharps. He'll never leave on his own and he's too good in a fight, even for the man who brought in Lijah Penne."

"That's murder you're talking. I just handed in my badge. I don't know if I could do it."

She stroked his cheek. "It wouldn't be murder. Not really."

"What do you mean?"

"It'd just be justice. He's murdered more than one."

"Who?"

"If I tell you and he finds out, he'll kill me."

"I won't tell anyone," Carson said.

"There's more, but you have to promise you'll kill him. If my daddy knew what he'd done to me, he'd try to kill him himself." She leaned back as if to gauge his reaction. "I fear he'd kill Daddy. He almost said as much. And I couldn't bear that." She leaned in to kiss him again.

He pulled back. "You mean?"

She nodded.

He stepped away from her. "That changes things."

"So, you'll do it?"

"It's a lot to ask. I need to think on it."

She pressed herself against his back. "Don't think too long. All this could be yours."

He turned toward her. "I don't think I can do it."

Her face hardened. "You're not the man I thought you were."

"I'd do it if I knew for sure he was a murderer. I'd be saving the court some time and money. I'd surely do it then."

She searched his face with her eyes. "Last year, he killed a whole family of nesters."

"Who?"

"A family of farmers driving across our range looking for a place to light."

"Why would he kill them?"

"They had a pert daughter, just blooming, and one of the boys told me Britt couldn't stop staring at her."

Carson covered his mouth with his hand and stared at the ground. After a few seconds, he looked up. "Where's the girl now?"

"Britt killed the whole family, except the girl, then he sent the rest of the men off to look for strays. After a time, the men heard a shot, and pretty soon, Britt rode up, looking like the cat that swallowed the canary."

"I'll do it," Carson said. "For you and for that poor girl and her family."

She pressed herself against him and ran her hands to the buttons on his trousers.

He grabbed her wrists.

She jerked them free and swatted his hand.

"It's not that I don't want to. Won't want to. But all this talk of killing, I don't think my heart or my head would be in it."

She leaned up and kissed his cheek. "I can wait until you've done what needs doing." She brushed her lips over his. "Don't make me wait too long."

CHAPTER twenty-seven

Though the feather bed was the softest he had ever slept on, Carson tossed and turned, his mind working hard to figure out what to do next. He dropped his feet to the cool, polished-pine floor and stepped to the window. A three-quarter moon lit the yard.

A red dot glowed and caught his eye. Britt, fully clothed, leaned against the bunkhouse, smoking a cigarette.

Carson glanced east. Daylight was still hours away. He returned to the bed and flopped back on top of the blankets. With only three more days, he had to act fast.

When someone knocked on his door, his eyes snapped open. "Who is it?"

"Bruna. Mr. Grimwald asked me to wake you."

"What time is it?"

"Quarter of six. The men will be eating soon."

"Thank you."

His heart pounded as he rushed into his clothes, buckled on his pistol, and bounded down the stairs, out the door, and across the yard to the cabin where the working men ate. As he entered, the men, lined up, waiting for the cook to start serving, turned as one.

"Good morning," Carson said with a smile. "I'm Carson Kettle. I'll be working with y'all."

Britt stepped through the door behind him. "Don't waste too much time getting to know Deputy Kettle. I doubt he'll be around for long. Out here, a man's gotta earn his keep."

The cook pushed open the door behind the long table and set down two cast-iron pots. He pulled back the lids, and the smell of flapjacks and bacon filled the room.

The men waited for Britt to step to the front of the line and fill his plate.

When Carson came to the pots, he found one half-burnt flapjack and two thin slices of bacon. It didn't matter; he had things on his mind besides food. He glanced around for an empty chair. Finding none, he leaned against the wall and ate his breakfast with his fingers.

When Britt finished eating, he said, "Horace, you take the crew over to Salt Creek and finish branding. Me and Remy gonna head over to Wiley's spring and show Deputy Kettle what it means to earn your keep on a working ranch."

As the men filed out, Carson dropped his plate into the tub with the others. "Should I saddle my horse?"

Britt smiled. "Nope. Go help Remy harness the mules."

Once the mules were harnessed, and the heavy farm wagon loaded with digging tools, Britt rode up. He grinned. "Best get a move on. Gonna be a scorcher later."

Remy placed his tarnished Yellowboy rifle under an old oilskin slicker behind the wagon seat, then climbed up beside Carson and took the lines.

When Britt rode off and was out of sight, Carson turned to Remy. "Where we going?"

"You ever get those soft hands dirty, Deputy?"

"I'm not a deputy anymore," Carson said, "And yes, I grew up on a farm."

"When's the last time you handled a shovel?"

Carson glanced at his soft palms still marked by half-healed blisters on the pads where his fingers met his palms. "I helped bury a man and his two boys, just a few days ago."

A small grove of cottonwoods and brush, an oasis in a sea of grass, burst into sight as they topped a small rise. Remy sighed and wiped his brow with his sleeve. "I don't know why the boss chose me to come with you. At least there's some shade and there won't be no branding fire adding to the heat."

"What are we doing?" Carson asked.

"Spring's all but stopped flowing. I reckon you and me and Britt gonna dig it out, see if we can fix it."

Britt trotted up behind them. "You're gonna have a bit of a rest today, Remy. The deputy's gonna do the digging. You're gonna tell him what to do."

Remy grinned. "What are you gonna do, boss?"

"I got some business in Eagle Flat."

Remy chuckled. "Senorita business, I reckon."

Britt laughed. "You're a smart man, Remy. That's why I like you. You don't let the deputy slack off. You hear?"

"No siree bob. I sure won't."

By the time the sun had almost reached its peak,

Carson's hands bled, and his back and shoulders ached. His shirt and pistol hung from a tree branch, but his boots were full of tepid, foul-smelling water, and his trousers were slick with red mud.

Remy sat in the shade of a cottonwood, scrapping black dirt from his fingernails with his belt knife.

"Could you hand me that bar?" Carson asked.

Remy glanced up, then returned to his nails.

Carson scrunched his toes to keep the mud from pulling off his boots. He splashed and sloshed his way to dry ground and picked up the heavy crowbar from where it leaned against the wagon. He wanted to talk to Remy before Britt returned. "We going to have lunch soon?"

Remy glanced up at the sun and nodded. "Soon."

Carson sighed with relief and turned back toward the wagon.

"Soon, but not yet."

Carson splashed back into the spring and rammed the flat end of the heavy bar between two boulders under the water. He pried and strained. The larger boulder shifted, and a tendril of clear water snaked up through the red sludge. "Help me! There's clean water coming from under this rock."

Remy sighed as he reached down and tugged off his boots and socks. "I reckon Britt and Mr. Grimwald'll be right glad if'n I can get this spring flowing cold and clean again." He stood and dropped his trousers and his faded red long handles and waded in beside Carson.

Remy's unwashed stink flooded past Carson's own hard-work-induced sweat and flooded his nose. He held his breath and pointed. "See it?"

Remy nodded and reached for the bar.

Using the smaller rock as a fulcrum, they pried the larger stone until a steady stream of clear water surged around them.

"There she is," Remy said.

"We've got to roll that rock back," Carson said between gritted teeth. "Can you hold it, while I get my hands under it?"

Remy pressed his chest over the bar. "Try now."

Carson leaned deeper and deeper into the water until it sloshed over his back. He felt with his fingers until he found the bottom edge of the flat stone. He squatted deeper, until only his mouth, nose, eyes, and forehead showed above the water. "On three."

Remy said. "Do it. I'm slipping."

"Okay. One, two, three." Carson pressed with his legs and lifted with everything he had, while Remy threw his own weight onto the bar.

The rock inched up, then as the bottom broke free of the mud, felt much lighter and Carson rolled it over.

Remy whooped and scooped clear water over his own head.

Carson dropped to his knees. Dropped his mouth into the clear flow and sucked in the cool sweet water that flooded into the spring. Once he'd drunk his fill, he looked up.

Remy grinned and splashed a handful of water toward him. "We did it! Well, mostly you did it."

Carson clapped a hand on Remy's shoulder. "We did it. I never could have moved that rock without you."

The warmth of the sun eased Carson's aching muscles as he lay back and closed his eyes. He would rest a minute, then eat the roast beef sandwich the cook had packed for him.

"Looks like you boys got her flowing," Britt said, jerking them both awake.

Remy sat up. "We just finished, Boss."

Britt grinned and pointed his pistol at Carson's half-dry socks and trousers draped over a tree branch and his boots hung upside down on the shove handle and the crowbar. "Looks like y'all been done a good while."

"Sorry, Boss," Remy said. "I didn't mean to fall asleep. I told Carson to wake me. Why you got your gun out?"

Britt smiled and held the pistol up. "This ain't for you Remy, unless you been talking to the deputy about some of the things we been doing round here."

"No, sir," Remy said. "I ain't said nothing." He pointed to the spring. "I even got in and helped him get her flowing."

Britt cocked his pistol and pointed it at Carson. "I ain't surprised the deputy's a little tired, after walking down to the pecan grove with Miss Patty last night. She do wear a man out."

Carson's cheeks burned. "We just talked."

"I know," Britt said. "Well, I suppose you did a little more than talk, but that don't matter," Britt said. "What matters is what she told you."

"She didn't tell me anything."

Britt shook his head. "You ain't a very good liar, Deputy. And you ain't too careful about who might be following you, when you got your nose full of the scent of a woman."

"You followed us?"

"Gotta protect what's mine. Me and Mr.

Grimwald halfway had us an agreement. I take care of things for him, and Miss Patty and this ranch'd be mine one day. I been doing my part, but it appears Miss Patty has other ideas."

Carson glanced at his pistol hanging from a branch near his trousers.

Britt motioned toward the pistol. "Fetch his pistol to me, Remy."

Remy climbed to his feet. "What's happening, Boss?"

"Fetch me his pistol."

Remy trotted over and grabbed Carson's gun belt from the branch stub it hung from.

Britt glanced down at his saddle horn. "Bring it over and hang it there."

"I still don't get it," Remy said.

"Not much to get, old friend. Miss Patty told the deputy here that I'm a killer."

Remy tugged on his ear and looked from Carson to Britt and back. "Not Miss Patty. She wouldn't tell what we done."

Britt grinned like a madman. "You old fool. She played you like she played all of us. She looks awful pretty, but she ain't."

Remy pinched the loose skin beneath his jaw. "Don't say that, Britt. She won't like you talking that way."

Sure Britt meant to kill him, Carson scanned the area. There was no good place to run. The small grove of trees around the spring would offer some short-term protection, but he would be trapped there, with no way to escape.

He looked straight at Remy. "She told me you were part of the killing, too," Carson said, "but she said it was Britt's fault. You help me and I'll put in a good word for you. Marshal Greer sets a lot of store in what I say."

Remy's eyes appeared blank, as if he weren't truly seeing as he glanced from Carson to Britt. "We should have said no. It wasn't right what we done, but she's the one told us to do it. Her and the old man. But they've always been good to me."

Britt grinned. "Right you are old friend." He swung his pistol and shot Remy in the forehead.

Remy's eyes opened wide in shock as he tumbled forward onto Carson's pistol.

Before Carson could react, Britt brought the Colt back to bear on his chest.

Carson needed to buy time. "I feel like a fool," he said, looking straight at Britt. "I guess it doesn't matter much now, but who else did Miss Patricia and her father have you kill?"

Britt grinned like a fool. "A lot of people. Though I didn't kill them all myself."

"The Burnetts?"

"Yes, sir."

"What about all the scalping?"

"That was Miss Patty's idea. Get the Indians fighting mad so the soldiers would have to kill them all or move them further west."

"Why scalp Mexicans and white people?"

Britt paused. "What do you mean?"

"Yost and his boys were scalping Mexicans and white people?"

Britt scratched his cheek with his gun barrel. "Black hair?"

Carson nodded.

Britt shook his head. "Can't trust no one these

days." He pointed the pistol at Carson's head. "Make your peace."

Carson glanced at his clothes. "At least let me die with my trousers on."

Britt thought for a few seconds, then motioned with the pistol. "Go on, then. I'd just have to dress you anyway, so's I could bring your scalped body back to the ranch. Don't get any ideas about running. There's nowhere to go. And you run, I'll make sure you die hard."

Carson nodded and motioned around them with his hand. "I can see there's nowhere to go. I just don't want to die in my underwear."

Britt motioned with his pistol. "Go on, then. Hurry up."

"I do have one more question."

Britt raised an eyebrow.

"Why Remy?"

Britt smiled. "You heard the way he was talking. Of all the boys except old Cliff, he thinks the most of Miss Patty. I got big plans, and with him talking that way, I couldn't risk him telling anyone what I done here or what I'm gonna do back at the ranch. Has to look like the Comanche done it."

Carson slipped on his trousers one leg at a time. Once he buttoned them and slipped on his shirt, he asked, "Can I put on my boots?"

Britt glanced at the boots hanging on the shovel and crowbar leaning against the wagon.

Carson dove behind the big cottonwood.

Britt's bullet slammed into the old tree.

Carson scrambled on his hands and feet, ducking and rolling deeper into the grove of trees and brush.

Britt's Colt barked again, but the bullet came nowhere near Carson.

"You make me come in there, I'll flay you and burn you, till you beg God to let you die, then I'll flay and burn you some more. You come out and I'll kill you quick."

Carson leaned in behind another big cottonwood and pulled the little derringer from his pocket. He said a silent prayer and begged God to let the little .41 short cartridges be dry enough to fire. Knowing the short range of the little pistol, he shouted, "You'll have to come in here and get me." He jumped to his feet and crashed through the brush, dove over a downed tree, and quieted his breathing. He glanced around and found a dry, broken branch with a jagged end. If the Derringer failed to fire it would be better than his bare hands.

CHAPTER twenty-eight

At first, Carson heard nothing. He cocked the Derringer and risked a peek over the log. Either Britt had not come into the grove or he was moving without making a sound.

A whiff of grass smoke floated by on the breeze.

Carson's heart leaped into his throat. Britt was trying to burn him out. That changed everything. The flames would force him from the trees and onto the open grasslands, where the longer range of Britt's Colt or Winchester would give him all the advantage.

Britt cursed. "Keep burning, damn you."

Carson licked his lips with cautious hope. Things were still pretty green. Maybe the flames wouldn't take hold and Britt would still have to come to him.

The sound of Britt dragging and snapping dry branches reached Carson as the smoke grew thicker.

As the flames roared and crackled, Britt whooped, then shouted, "Might as well come out. I got things burning good."

Carson held his breath as the smoke around him grew dense. He rose to his knees. Through the smoke, flames already rose from the years of dry leaves and grass on the floor of the little forest and licked at the green leaves and branches of the old cottonwoods.

His eyes filled with tears as he rose to his feet. He crouched low and ran from the flames and smoke toward the far side of the trees. But what then? He'd be flushed into the open.

He cut hard to his left. He remembered the time his father had shown him how a lightning strike had started a grass fire back home. The fire had started narrow, just a few feet wide, and widened, bit by bit, in a wedge, until the blackened ground was a mile wide where the flames had died on the banks of the river.

Praying the smoke and fire would cover his movements, Carson sprinted in a wide circle that would take him back to the spring. If Britt had already gone around to wait for him to flush from the trees, Remy's rifle was behind the seat of the wagon. If Britt were still waiting near the spring, hopefully he could find enough cover to get close enough to use the Derringer.

As he drew near the north side of the grove, the smoke thinned. He rubbed his eyes, crept to the edge of trees, and crawled under the low branches of a clump of sweetshrub.

Britt and his horse were gone.

Carson stayed in the cover of the trees until he had a clear, straight path to the wagon. He hesitated and looked both ways, then sprinted across the thirty yards to the wagon, dropped the branch, and threw himself up and over the side. He pocketed the Derringer and dragged out the old slicker. Remy's rifle was gone.

"You looking for this?" Britt said.

Carson snapped his eyes toward Britt's voice.

Grinning like he'd just won a prize at the fair, Britt rode toward him, pointing Remy's Yellowboy. "You must think I'm stupid. Remy's been sticking this Winchester behind that seat for as long as I've known him."

Carson shrugged his shoulders as he inched his hand toward the Derringer in his pocket. "Now what?"

Britt chuckled. "You ever see what the Comanche do to their captives?"

Carson shook his head.

He gestured with Remy's rifle. "Get down off that wagon. You're about to find out."

Carson's fingers found the Derringer, just as his first foot hit the ground.

"Now come on around here and lay on your belly," Britt said.

Carson eased himself down to one knee and then the other.

Britt's smile fled, and his cheeks reddened. "I said, come around here."

Using the wagon as cover, Carson slid the Derringer from his pocket and eased back the hammer.

"Now!" Britt shouted.

Carson waited without moving.

"You hear me? I said come around here."

Carson stared straight ahead.

"You'll soon have a lot to say, boy," Britt shouted. He started his horse around the wagon tongue. He was less than ten feet away when he raised the Yellowboy, and less than three feet away when he swung it toward Carson's head.

Carson tumbled and rolled to one side as the rifle barrel swished past his ear. He pointed and pulled the trigger. The little pistol bucked in his hand, and the forty-one-caliber bullet tore through Britt's knee and deep into his thigh.

Britt yelped as his horse spun away from Carson's shot. He swung the Yellowboy with one hand and was about to pull the trigger when Carson's second shot drove through the muscle and ribs under his arm, piercing his lung, but stopping short of his heart. He jerked and the bullet from the Yellowboy slammed into the side of the wagon.

Carson rolled and came to his feet with the jagged stick in his hands.

Britt fought his horse back around and tried to lever the Yellowboy with one hand.

Carson yelled and slammed the branch deep into the big man's belly and drove him from his horse. The Yellowboy clattered to the ground, and Carson dove onto it and rolled away, with it in his hands. He levered in a round and turned to fire before Britt could draw his pistol.

Britt sat on his heels, both of his hands on the branch protruding from his belly. He met Carson's eyes. Bright blood bubbling from his nose and mouth. His words burbled through the blood. "I reckon she's all yours, Mr. Carson Kettle. Enjoy."

"It's Deputy Kettle," Carson said, as Britt tumbled onto his side and choked out his last breath.

*****

Carson drove the mules into the yard with Britt's big buckskin and white pinto tied behind the wagon.

Patricia ran from the house. A smile lit her face, then faded as she peered over the side of the wagon. "Remy?" She glared at Carson. "Why Remy?"

Carson turned and pointed at Britt's body. "He did it. He said, he was afraid Remy would warn you about what he planned to do to you and your father."

A tear formed in the corner of her eye as she touched Carson's leg. "I liked old Remy. He was here when I was born." She looked toward the pecan grove. "I suppose he deserves a spot in the family plot."

"What about Britt?"

She spat on the ground. "Leave him out on the prairie for the buzzards as far as I care."

Carson met her eyes. "Maybe you can have one of the other men do the burying. I need to talk to you and your father."

She nodded. "Tell Jose to do it. I guess you're the foreman now."

"I'll find Jose, but I need some answers before I take on that job."

Her eyes darkened. "What did he tell you?"

Carson shook the reins and started the mules. "I'll come inside as soon as I find Jose."

CHAPTER twenty-nine

Carson stood before the heavy wooden door and waited for someone to answer his knock. When Patricia said, "Just come in," he took a deep breath to steady his vibrating body and stepped inside.

The old man sat in his wheelchair with a blanket over his lap. He glanced at Carson, then looked away and raised his glass to his lips.

Patricia poured a full glass of her father's fine whiskey and held it out. "You look like you need this." When Carson took it, she picked up her own half-full glass and raised it. "To the future."

Carson clinked her glass with his, then extended his glass toward Mr. Grimwald.

The old man glared and pulled a cocked pistol from beneath the blanket.

"Daddy's not happy with us," Patricia said.

"She begged me not to shoot you as soon as you walked through the door. She said you'd explain things together. I don't see what you two could say, but I'm listening."

Carson locked his eyes on the black hole in the end of the gun barrel. "Britt told Remy he planned to kill you both and take the ranch. That's why he murdered him. He tried to kill me too, but I got him first."

Mr. Grimwald took a big swallow. "I find that hard to believe. Britt's been here a long time and he and I have been talking about the future. Why would he do that?"

Carson glanced at Patricia and hesitated. "He saw Patricia and I out walking. He followed and listened to us talking."

Patricia's eyes opened wide.

"He said if he couldn't have her, no one would. He'd kill her first, and he knew you'd never let that go."

Mr. Grimwald looked up at his daughter. "That sounds like Britt. Why couldn't you just go along with my plans. Takes a strong hand to run this outfit. And Britt was as tough as they come." He cast his angry eyes on her. "You know I built this place. Tore it from the wilderness with these two hands, and I'm still in charge here."

She touched her father's shoulder. "Put the gun down, Daddy. You won't be shooting anyone today. You raised me like the son you never had. I could never let a man, well, I mean, other than you, run things here, and Britt couldn't, wouldn't accept that. He told Remy that once we were married, he'd break me."

Mr. Grimwald took another drink and wiped his lips with the back of his hand. "What about you, young man? How do you feel about Patricia being in charge?"

Carson raised his glass and took a tiny sip. He needed a moment to gather his thoughts but couldn't afford to let the whiskey cloud them. "When my Pa went off to war, my Ma ran things. I did as she asked, and things worked out just fine."

Patricia smiled.

"But I'm not sure I'm staying," Carson said.

Patricia's smile fled. "Why not?"

Britt said some things.

"What things?"

"Things about what's been going on around here."

Mr. Grimwald shook his head. "I find that hard to believe. Why would he tell you anything?"

"He was dying and maybe he needed to get it off his chest, but I think he thought it would turn me against you both."

"What did he tell you?" Patricia asked.

Carson looked her in the eyes. "If you want me to stay, you'll trust me and tell me right now what you've done to the farmers and the others. Otherwise, I'll pack my bag, forget every word he said, and head west."

Patricia looked at her father.

He shook his head. "There's nothing to tell. I'm sure you're right. Britt was always a vengeful boy. And if he couldn't have Patricia, he'd want to turn you against her. You'd best pack your things."

"Daddy. No."

"That's my final word on it. We don't know this boy and we don't owe him anything." He turned to Carson. "If you want to stay the night, you can sleep in the bunkhouse with the men, but you might want to just ride out. Some of those boys thought the sun rose and set with old Britt."

Carson's body felt like it was shrinking in on itself and he struggled to take a breath. He couldn't leave now. They would just continue killing and stirring things up until they owned enough of the country and had enough money that no one would question them. He had to think of a way to get them to admit what they'd done.

He stepped around in front of the old man. "Remy confirmed everything Britt said, and I don't give two hoots about what you've done, but I won't stay on if you don't trust me."

Mr. Grimwald looked into Carson's eyes. "You haven't done anything to prove yourself to us. We barely know you. Go on up and pack your things."

Patricia glanced at Carson, then gripped her father's shoulder. "I trust him, Daddy. He's done things for me. Things no stranger would do?"

The old man raised his head and narrowed his eyes. "What do you mean? What things?"

She emptied her glass. "I asked him to kill Britt."

Her father jerked like he'd been shot. "You what?"

"I asked him to kill Britt."

The old man set the Colt in his lap, grabbed the wheels of his chair and spun it around. "Bruna! Come and take me to my room."

"Britt threatened me," Patricia said. "He said if I didn't do just as he told me, he'd cut you up and feed you to the dogs."

Mr. Grimwald's hands fell from the wheels and the chair stopped. "It's alright, Bruna. You go on back to the kitchen." He slowly turned the chair and met Patricia's eyes. He stared for what seemed to Carson like minutes then broke away and looked at the blanket covering his useless legs. "He said that?"

"That and more," she said "And he used me and hurt me."

The old man looked broken. "Why didn't you tell me?"

"Britt would have killed you and I couldn't bear to lose you."

Mr. Grimwald sighed and looked up at Carson. "If we tell you things, there's no turning back. Once you know the truth. You're bound to us, for as long as we're all here."

Carson looked from Mr. Grimwald to Patricia and back. If all went well, they would not be here for long. He nodded. "Alright, I accept your terms."

Mr. Grimwald emptied his glass. "Those Johnny-come-lately nesters don't deserve anything out here. They waited back east for us to fight off the Indians and make the place safe, before they dared come sneaking in. And what do they take? The springs and the best bottom land. They're common thieves and they deserve everything they get."

"What about the Indians?" Carson asked.

"Just look at them," the old man said, spittle blasting from his lips. "You've seen all that grass north of the river, and other than feeding a few scrub ponies, it's all going to waste while the savages suckle on the government's teat. Won't hurt them one bit to move further west. There's enough grass out there for their ponies and the government beef and beans will taste the same no matter where they live."

Carson looked at Patricia. "Yost and his men?"
She nodded.

"Did you know they were killing anyone they found with black hair? Mexicans, even white folk? Bella's father?"

She looked at the floor, then back up at Carson. "I didn't know. That was never our intent, but I read history and there are unintended casualties in any war. Always have been. Always will be. Any worthy goal comes at a cost. Sometimes it's a cost higher than we want to pay but pay it we must."

*****

Carson lay on the soft bed staring at the ceiling. He had chewed on the problem in his mind for over an hour. He had to get away. There was no way for him to arrest the Grimwalds and get them back to Fort Sill and then to Fort Smith. Not with a bunkhouse full of loyal men.

He would enlist Marty and Major Kinsey and his troopers to help.

Someone knocked on his door.

His heart raced. The handle turned. He picked up his Colt from the bedside table.

The door handle bumped against the wooden chair he had wedged there. Patricia whispered, "Carson?"

He lay silent.

"Carson. It's me. Let me in."

He lay without moving until her footsteps faded away and her door clicked shut.

He lay there for another hour, then slid out of bed and belted on his Colt. He eased the chair from beneath the handle, cracked the door, and peeked out into the hallway, ducked back in, picked up his boots with one hand and his saddlebags with the other, and slipped out into the hallway.

After pausing a moment to listen, he crept along the hallway and down the stairs. He was almost to the front door when the four clicks of a Colt revolver cocking, froze him.

A match scratched and Mr. Grimwald appeared in the light, his blanket pushed aside and his pistol in hand. He touched the match flame to a candle on the low table beside him and smiled. "My Patricia's too trusting sometimes, but I suppose this will be a good lesson for her." He motioned Carson back toward the stairs with his pistol, then shouted. "Patricia. Wake up. I need you down here. Now!"

Patricia's door slammed open, and she skidded to a stop at the top of the stairs. She stared at Carson and the saddlebags and the boots in his hands. Rage filled her face. "Kill him!" she shouted.

"Let's take him outside first," her father said. "I don't want the mess on the floor."

"Kill him, now!" she said.

Her father shook his head. "Go wake up the men. I'd like to see him swing."

"You won't shoot him, I will," she said. She turned and ran back toward her room.

When Mr. Grimwald glanced up at her departing form, Carson threw his saddlebags at the old man's head, dove onto the floor, and slid across the polished planks.

Grimwald's shot slammed into the wall behind where Carson had just stood.

Before he could fire again, Carson grabbed a wheel of Mr. Grimwald's chair and heaved up, spilling the crippled man against the table and onto the floor.

The candle fell over. The flame sputtered then caught on the molten wax that spilled onto the lace doily on the table.

Carson rolled and fired at the same time as Mr. Grimwald. Grimwald's shot creased the floor, but Carson's thunked into flesh.

The old man grunted at the impact. Carson kept rolling.

Mr. Grimwald's next shot, again, slammed into the pine boards. Carson shot at the stab of flame, and Mr. Grimwald's pistol clattered to the floor.

Patricia fired her pistol from the top of the stairs. Her bullet tore through the fleshy knot of Carson's shoulder and his Colt clattered from his hand.

She bounded down the stairs two at a time, glanced at her father then turned her hate-filled eyes on Carson.

For the second time in as many days, the Derringer saved Carson's life as the little forty-one-caliber bullet tore through her elegant throat.

Carson glanced from Patricia to her father. Neither moved. Flame now licked up the ornate wallpaper toward the ceiling. He had to get out of the house and away before the hands got here. He pocketed the Derringer and reached for his Colt. Pain shot up his neck and down his arm, but his bloody fingers gripped the big pistol. He scooped up his boots and saddlebags with his left hand and started for the back door.

Bruna stood, wide-eyed, her hand over her mouth, in the doorway to the kitchen. She screamed as he brushed by her.

He paused. "Get out, Bruna. Before it burns down."

Someone banged on the front door. Carson pushed past Bruna and sprinted to the back door.

Horace shouted, "Mr. Grimwald?"

"Fire!" Bruna shouted. "Help! He shot them! Fire!"

Carson skirted the house and peeked into the yard. Ranch hands poured from the bunkhouse into the barn, then emerged carrying buckets and began a bucket brigade, scooping water from the large trough in the corral and handing them from man to man.

Staying as much as he could to the shadows, Carson crept around the perimeter of the yard and sneaked into the barn. He holstered his Colt and struggled to pull on his boots with his left hand. He flexed his right arm. Pain racked him, but everything seemed to work. He'd tend to it later.

He pulled his sorrel from a stall and led him to the saddle tree in the corner. Light from the burning house flickered into the barn. He swung his saddle onto the sorrel's back, tightened the cinch, and threw his saddlebags over the horse's neck, in front of the saddle horn. He mounted, jerked his Winchester from its scabbard, and ignoring the pain, jacked in a round. He eased the sorrel toward the door. If the men were all fighting the fire, he would sneak around the barn and away before they saw him; if not, he would fight.

Horace, pistol in hand, burst into the barn.

The sorrel shied back.

Horace fired and missed.

Carson pushed the sorrel forward, extended the rifle until it almost touched the ranch hand, fired with one hand, and hit Horace square in the chest.

Ducking low, he drove the sorrel through the barn door and turned him right.

Flames shooting up through the roof of the big house lit the yard like it was midday.

"There he is," Bruna shouted from the yard.

A young cowboy fired a wild shot.

Carson drove his heels into the sorrel and snapped a shot at the shooter. In two strides the big sorrel carried him to, and around, the corner of the big barn.

Fifty yards behind the barn, he stopped the sorrel and shouted, "This is Deputy U.S. Marshal Carson Kettle." He paused until the men in the yard stopped shouting. "I'll be back tomorrow with a posse. Anyone still here will be arrested for murder."

He ducked low and drove the sorrel north toward the Red River and Fort Sill.

CHAPTER thirty

Bella set a wooden crate onto the red dust of the road. She bent at the waist and sucked in air, until her breathing slowed a little.

Mr. Cadwallader trotted down the hill toward her. "What doest thou have there?"

"Books," she said. "My father's books."

"Let me help thee," he said. "I have some good news."

They picked up the crate and lugged it the last few yards to her room. Once they had set it down, he said, "I've found a wonderful Christian home for Perdita among the Cherokee. I thought you might want to spend some time with her before they leave on the morrow."

Bella smiled. "I would. Perhaps after supper?"

He bowed and touched his hat. "Until then."

Using a table knife, she had borrowed from the dining hall, Bella pried the lid from the crate and set it aside. She pulled out the top book, her family's Bible. She picked up the pen she had taken from the major's office. She had been sure he wouldn't mind her slipping in when no one was there, just for the pen and ink and nothing else. The letter Carson had written to her, the letter she now knew she wasn't meant to see, unless Carson failed to return, lay on the table beside the inkwell. Unsure what the letter meant or how she should react, she turned to the task at hand. She opened the Bible to the pages at the front of the old book and ran her fingers down a stiff page.

A tear formed in her eye as she traced her finger over the ornate script marking her mother's death. She dipped the pen and added her father's name and the date of his death.

She touched her belly. "One day this Bible will be yours." She crossed herself. "God willing."

She blew over the ink, until the sheen faded, then closed the heavy book and set it aside.

She reached into the crate and pulled out one book after another, each volume precious enough to her father to bring west. And now precious to her. Tears flowed down her cheeks as she fondled the books and read a few words from each one.

Halfway through the stack, she reached for an ancient, leather-bound tome. Something rattled when she picked it up. Flipping it open, she discovered the pages had been hollowed out, and in the hollow, she found thirty $20 gold eagles.

*****

A mile north of the Grimwald ranch buildings, Carson stopped the sorrel on a high spot of ground. Flames shot into the sky from the burning ranch house, but there was no sign of pursuit.

He ran his fingers up the blood-soaked sleeve of his shirt. Blood ran from the front and back of the wound. He flexed the muscle and lifted his arm. More blood flowed. Already, he felt lightheaded. With his left hand, he pulled his clean shirt from his saddle bags. Using his teeth, he started a tear in one sleeve, and ripped it from the rest of the shirt and pressed it as far as he could stand into each side of the wound.

Sweat poured from his forehead as he glanced back at the ranch. Already, the flames had diminished. The big house was gone, and likely with it, Patricia and her father. He remembered her elegant face and the taste of her lips and tongue but felt only sadness. There was nothing pretty about her. Bella, on the other hand, was beautiful.

By the time he approached Fort Sill, the sun warmed his back and the blood on his shoulder had dried into the shirt sleeve. He passed a Cherokee couple, with a babe in arms and three little children, walking along the road. He tried to greet them, but all that came from his dry throat was a raspy croak.

The couple looked at his face, then glanced at his bloody arm and hurried on.

As he approached the stables, something was wrong. At first his swirling brain couldn't figure it out, then it hit him like a hammer. There was only one wagon.

He drove the sorrel through the open doors of the stable and pushed him down the long alleyway. Cavalry mounts, tied in tie stalls, glanced over their shoulders, and swished their tails as he rode by. The stalls where Trajetta's heavy horses had been stabled, stood empty.

Blackness closed in around his vision and he tumbled from the saddle.

When he opened his eyes, Marty laughed and said, "There you are."

Nancy wiped a damp cloth over his forehead.

He looked up at a whitewashed ceiling. "Where am I?"

"Don't you remember?" Marty asked.

Carson dug into his memory. "Last I remember, I was...." He cast wild eyes around the room and tried to sit up. "Where's Bella?"

<<<<>>>>

Thank you for reading my little tale. If you would like to read the next Carson Kettle adventure, you can find it here.:
https://www.amazon.com/~/e/B07JNZ79WD

Afterward

May 25, 2021

Once again, I thank you for sharing this adventure of mine. I hope it brought you pleasure and made the hours you spent with us a little brighter.

It's been a long year with all the fear and restrictions surrounding Covid 19, but it feels like we are finally seeing the light at the end of this long tunnel.

Up here in the north country, there are still some covid restrictions in place and many rodeos and other social events are still being canceled. Since spending Christmas in Texas with our youngest two daughters, we haven't strayed too far from home.

Almost before we got home, we missed the simple freedoms we had in Texas, little things like going to the movies and eating out. We saw the movie 'News of the World' while we were in Stephenville. It's a nice old west story about a Texas man who agrees to accompany a young girl, who had been taken captive by the Kiowa, to her family in the Texas Hill country. He makes his living traveling from town-to-town reading news articles to people yearning to hear about interesting things going on in the rest of the world.

I enjoyed the movie so much; I came home and bought the book. With a few exceptions, the movie follows the book, and I recommend either one.

Speaking of news, I sometimes long for the days where I got my news delivered to the door by a neighbor boy. My small-town newspaper was full of local events and the happenings in our rural community. Now I have to catch myself and get outside before I tumble down the internet rabbit hole of death and destruction from all around this big, wide world.

Instead of watching the news or traveling, my wife and I have been focusing on exercise and healthy eating. We've each lost over 50 pounds. I'm sure my old rope horse appreciates that.

Our youngest daughter finished her college rodeo career this spring. She and her young mare did well, but now it's time for her to go on to new and exciting career and rodeo adventures.

Here at home, we've got some cattle out on pasture and we're looking forward to some good, grass-finished beef in the fall.

Carson is already whispering to me about his next adventure. I'm sure it will include Bella and Marty and maybe even Gate.

It's almost June. We've had a much-needed rain over the last few days. The lilacs and cherry trees are blossoming, and the cattle are slick and fat. Overall, life is good.

Until next time, all the best to you and yours.

Wyatt

Printed in Great Britain
by Amazon